Praise for

Son of Fletch . . .

"HEALTH WARNING TO MYSTERY READERS: *Son of Fletch* stopped me from sleeping last night. It must be the wittiest, twistiest story I've read this year, and consequently very addictive."
                                    —**Peter Lovesey**

"WHAT SHEER PLEASURE, a new Fletch novel from the smart, acerbic, one-of-a-kind Gregory Mcdonald . . . The dialogue snaps and fizzes, the plot moves with swift efficient elegance, and Mr. Mcdonald's wise and knowing spirit informs all."
                                    —**Peter Straub**

"*Son of Fletch* takes the Fletch saga to another level . . . a real winner."   —**Morris Dees, cofounder, Southern Poverty Law Center**

"THE DIALOGUE IS FAST, FUNNY AND FEARFULLY CLEVER . . . better than most crime fiction out there . . . a heck of a lot of fun."
                                    —*Trenton Times*

"READERS WILL GLADLY SUCCUMB to Mcdonald's laconic wit and smooth pacing . . . Fletch, Carrie, and the enterprising Jack . . . are all fully dimensioned characters who rate readers' attention and applause."   —*Publishers Weekly*

Also by Gregory Mcdonald

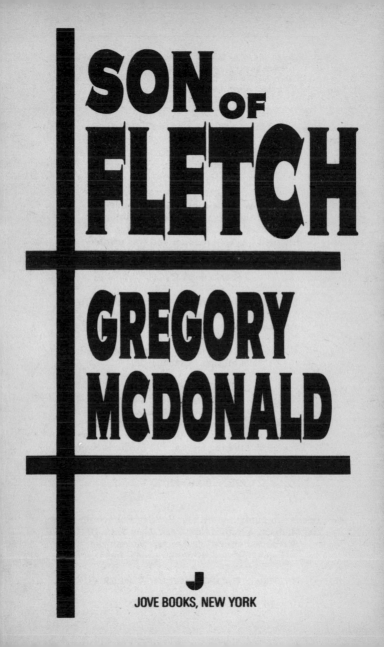

SON OF FLETCH

GREGORY MCDONALD

JOVE BOOKS, NEW YORK

This Jove Book contains the complete
text of the original hardcover edition.
It has been completely reset in a typeface
designed for easy reading and was printed
from new film.

SON OF FLETCH

A Jove Book / published by arrangement with
the author

PRINTING HISTORY
G.P. Putnam's Sons edition / September 1993
Jove edition / October 1994

ISBN: 0-515-11470-7

A JOVE BOOK®
Jove Books are published by The Berkley Publishing Group,
200 Madison Avenue, New York, New York 10016.
JOVE and the "J" design are trademarks
belonging to Jove Publications, Inc.

PRINTED IN THE UNITED STATES OF AMERICA

10 9 8 7 6 5 4 3 2 1

chapter 1

"Mister Fletcher?"

In the hard rain, Fletch had stopped the Jeep at the roadblock on the narrow county road. It was raining so hard he and Carrie had almost failed to see the sputtering warning flares as they came down the twisting, rock-walled road through the gap.

When the Jeep was stopped in front of the two county police cars parked as a wedge facing them, their headlights lit, a great bulk of a man wearing a yellow slicker and a dark, wide-brimmed hat lumbered toward them. He was lit by the Jeep's headlights but more backlit by the high beams of the police cars.

"Ha!" Carrie had said. "Fletch, I told you not to leave your popcorn bucket on the floor of the movie theater! They're out lookin' for you, now they've cotched you, and they'll put you under the jailhouse for sure."

"Who is that?" Fletch asked.

The rain pounding on the canvas roof of the Jeep made them speak loudly.

"Rondy," Carrie answered. "You know him. His uncle is Biggie Wilson. You been huntin' with him, that time you all treed the Carter boy 'cause he has the natural smell of possum."

Fletch opened the Jeep's door, as that was easier than unzipping the window.

"Hiya, Rondy. How's your Uncle Big Stuff?"

"He's just fine, Mister Fletcher." Rondy flashed his light around the interior of the Jeep. He leaned to look directly behind their seats. "Evenin', Carrie. You folks doin' all right?"

Carrie said, "Happier than worms wrigglin' in warm mud."

Rain was pouring off the brim of the deputy's hat. "Plenty of warm mud around."

"What's happening, Rondy?" Carrie leaned forward in the passenger seat and spoke across Fletch. "The sheriff misplace his spectacles again?"

"Some villains decided to take themselves a little vacation from the federal penitentiary up in Kentucky, Carrie."

"Can't blame 'em," Fletch said. "We've been advertising Tennessee as a vacation spot. *Take yourselves off to Tennessee.* Isn't that the slogan?"

"We've been told to welcome tourists all right, Mister Fletcher. It's just that we're concerned these particular fellows, being wards of the government, a federal responsibility, might stay out so late they

o〇ooo〇ooo〇o

just might miss their breakfasts."

"Can't let that happen."

"No, sir. They left home without any pocket money, is what has us worried."

Fletch smiled. "Armed and dangerous?"

"We don't know if they're armed yet. If not, they sure will be soon enough. Dangerous for sure."

Also dressed in yellow slickers, wide-brimmed hat, black rubber boots, carrying a flashlight, Sheriff Rogers came up and joined Deputy Wilson at the Jeep's door.

The jeans on Fletch's left leg were getting soaked.

"Mister Fletcher. Miss Carrie."

"Howdy, Sheriff," Carrie said. "Don't Francie let you take a shower-bath at home anymore?"

"Says I keep leavin' wet towels on the bathroom floor. So she sends me out every time there's a hard rain. She's been complainin' about wet towels on the floor thirty-two years now." The sheriff grinned. "Funny how some women never change."

"Nor should we," sniffed Carrie.

"How long since you all been gone from the farm?"

"Few hours," Fletch answered. "Went to St. Ives, had supper, saw a movie. Left home about what, five-fifteen?"

"You got guns at home, Mister Fletcher?"

"Sure."

"Anywhere an intruder could find them?"

"Sure."

"Loaded?"

"No. The shells and cartridges are kept separate."

"That's good. Maybe we should send Rondy here home with you."

oOooOooOo

Rondy frowned at the little space in the back of the Jeep.

"We'll be all right. How many villains are you lookin' for tonight?"

"Four." The sheriff fished a wet piece of paper out of his pocket and held his flashlight on it under the Jeep's roof. "One murderer, one attempted murderer, one kidnapper, and one serving heavy time on drug charges."

"Shoot," Fletch said. "I thought Rondy said these were bad dudes. You have their names there?"

Rainwater ran down the sheriff's face despite his wide-brimmed hat. "Kriegel, Faoni, Leary, and Moreno." The sheriff accented the first syllable of the last name. Putting the paper back into his pocket, he said, "Can't figure why they're coming through here."

"Headed south, I suppose," Fletch said. "Alabama border. Lose themselves in Florida."

"Except they've drifted sideways," the sheriff said. "This isn't a direct route to anywhere for them, far as I can figure."

"How do you know they're here?"

"Told they were comin' this way, for sure. Then Ms. Mobley spotted them running along the ridge just before sunset." The sheriff waved toward the west. "Guess we can believe her, all right." In her sixties, Mary Ann Mobley was considered the sharpest-eyed hunter in the county. "Couldn't get to 'em, of course, in all this dampness." The sheriff craned to look at the Jeep's shifts. "This a four-wheel drive, Fletch?"

"Yes, sir."

o⊂∞⊂∞⊃∞⊃o

"Mind if we borrow your Jeep, Fletch? We'll start by patrolling your farm."

"Not at all. You're welcome to it."

"Trouble is, I really need Rondall here. There are just the two of us, two cars. Maybe I'll radio in and have a couple of deputies stop by your farm on their way out from town. They can pick up your Jeep, patrol your farm, then come find us."

"That will be fine."

"Got gas?"

"Filled up in St. Ives."

"We'll appreciate it."

"So will I." Fletch put the Jeep in first gear.

"Be real careful going into your place. Unless they're traveling faster than they have been, there's a large chance they're down there somewhere near or on your farm. Sorry I can't spare Rondy to go with you."

"We'll be fine. Not to worry." Fletch closed the Jeep's door.

Slowly he drove between the blinding headlights of the police cars.

Already Carrie was picking her fingers. "Well, I'm worried. A little bit."

"About what?" Fletch asked.

Carrie looked toward her rain-streaked plastic window. "Four villains peekin' out of the bushes at us."

Fletch said, "Around here we've got coyotes, wolves, bobcats, panthers, and snakes."

"And a bear." Carrie insisted she ran into a bear between the barns one dark night. She hadn't lingered to collect evidence it really was a bear.

"You're not all that afraid of snakes, bobcats, and bears, are you?"

"Animals make sense, Fletch," Carrie said. "It's the humans you can't trust worth a patootie."

"Should I stay here?"

"Absolutely not." Using the four-wheel drive, Fletch had driven up the old dirt timber road at the back of the farm. Lights out, he drove along the top of the hill behind the farmhouse. He stopped just inside the edge of the woods. "These dudes want the Jeep. And they want you. I'd rather you stay with me."

"You don't care as much about the Jeep?"

"Not as much. I'm going to let the counties use it, aren't I?" A few months before, two of the county's cars had smashed into each other, in a parking lot.

In the hard rain they walked together down the hill just inside the line of trees. Even though they were slipping and sliding on the wet hillside, Carrie took his hand. "Maybe the bobcats will get 'em," she said. "Maybe that panther you saw the other night will tear 'em apart like lettuce leaves."

"If you don't hush," Fletch said, "we might as well be driving up the driveway honking the horn and going in the side door singing 'Three Coynes in a Barroom.'"

"First time I've thought kindly of rattlesnakes," Carrie said.

When they got just above the house, Fletch said, "You might stay here now. Give me time to case the joint."

oᏅ⧭oᏅᏅoᏅ⧭oᏅo

"Here? This is about the place we saw the black wolf go into the woods last fall."

"You think he's still here?"

"Might could be."

"There's plenty for a wolf to eat out here without taking a snack out of you. It's the hungry, two-legged variety who think food only grows in refrigerators we need to worry about right now."

"I don't have a gun," Carrie said. "What do I do if the wolf comes by?"

"What you charmin' Tennesseans always do."

"What's that?"

"Say, 'Hydy, Mister Wolf. How's your pa?' "

"Which paw will I be askin' about in this case? Right, left, front, back?"

"If you hush your mouth, at least the humans won't know you're here."

He climbed over the white board fence. Crouching, he circumnavigated the house. He peered through the windows into every room on the first floor. Throughout the house there were baseboard safety lights.

Behind the house, he opened the door to the smokehouse. In the dark, rain pounding on the aluminum roof, he found the pipe end, about six inches long, an inch wide, he had left there that afternoon after making a repair in the pump house.

He placed the white PVC pipe on the walk leading from the side of the house to the barns, just outside the study. It would be visible on the path once the lights in the study were lit.

Then he entered the house through the back door, went from room to room and upstairs turning on

○c◯○◯◯○c◯◯○

lights. He took the handgun from his bathroom closet and loaded it. There was no sensible place to carry
it in his sopping shirt and jeans, so he kept it in his
right hand.

Openly he went back across the backyard in the
rain.

"Okay," he quietly said over the fence. "You can
come out now. All yee, all yee, home be."

"I'm not here."

"Oh?" He could not see her in the dark woods.

"A panther carried me off by the foot, all you
care."

Wet blond hair streaming down her face, she
climbed over the fence.

"No sign they've even been here. Even the porridge
hasn't been touched."

"Long as they leave my pickled beets alone."

In the kitchen, Carrie said, "Me for a shower. A
warm shower. You too?"

"Guess I'll wait until you're finished."

"Will you come upstairs with me?"

"There are no panthers upstairs. I already looked."

He got a can of tuna fish out of the cupboard.

She asked, "You hungry?"

"No. Come to think of it, let me go upstairs for the
shotgun. Then I'd like you to go into the living room,
turn out the lights, and wait for me."

"Oh." Wet and cold, she shivered. "The Jeep."

Leaving Carrie standing alone with the loaded
shotgun in a corner of the dark living room, Fletch
jogged up the slippery hill. There was no question
whatsoever in his mind that if she were confronted
with an intruder, Carrie would not only shoot, she

would shoot as well as she normally did, which was very well indeed. Without a blink of hesitation, if armed, calmly she would blow the head off anyone who messed with her, or hers. In his years in the southern part of the United States, Fletch had come to know and respect the Southern country woman considerably in this way. Distinctly Carrie was a Southern country woman.

Thinking it would be safer, Fletch drove the Jeep back along the timber road, down to the hardtop road, down it to the driveway, and up it. He left the Jeep in the carport, with the truck and the station wagon.

In the dining room, he said into the dark living room, "If you don't shoot me, just maybe I'll live to give you a kiss."

"What will you give me if I do shoot you?"

"The job of having to dig a big hole somewhere."

"Are you alone?"

The intelligence of the question impressed him. "Except for Za-Za and Fifi."

"Don't joke."

"I'm alone," Fletch said.

"Prove it."

"All escaped convicts are chickens."

"Okay."

In the bedroom, staying nearer to the door to the house than to the bathroom door, so he could hear over the sound of the shower, Fletch pulled off his boots and his wet clothes. He put on his bathrobe.

"All done." Carrie came out of the bathroom with a towel wrapped around her head.

"Are you going to use the hair dryer?"

oՕ∘∘Օ∘∘Օo

"I have to."

"I'll wait."

When she was done, he left her in the bedroom with the handgun and took a quick, warm shower himself.

"Okay." He put the shotgun on the floor next to Carrie's side of the bed, away from the bedroom door. "Is this good for you?"

"Fine."

He changed into fresh jeans, shirt, and running shoes. "I'll be downstairs."

"Are you going to sit up all night?"

"Maybe."

In the kitchen, he picked up the phone and listened. He tried a few numbers.

The phone was dead.

He mixed the tuna fish with chopped onion, celery, and mayonnaise. He lightly toasted two pieces of bread. He put the light toast on a plate, heaped the tuna mix on the toast, and spread Swiss cheese on the tuna. He put the plate into the oven. He did not turn on the oven.

Then he went into the study.

He opened the French door behind his desk.

With his back to the door, he sat at his desk, apparently relaxed.

He slid the handgun under some loose papers on his desk.

Outside, the storm raged. The rain was deafening. The wind moved a paper on his desk. After the warm day, the breeze cooled off the study quickly.

Fletch did not have long to wait.

oᴄ⃝ooᴄ⃝ooᴄ⃝o

It was only a few minutes when he felt the small, round object pressed just below his left ear.

A voice behind him said, "Don't move."

Fletch said, "Hydy, son. How's your ma?"

o◯ooo◯ooo◯o

chapter 2

Careful not to move, Fletch said, "Son, put down that PVC!" He chuckled.

Behind him, a young man's voice asked, "What's a PVC?"

"In this instance," Fletch answered, "I mean that piece of white, plastic pipe, six inches long, one inch in diameter you're holding in your left hand."

Fletch continued to feel the pressure against his head, behind, below his left ear. The voice said, "It's a gun barrel."

"Couldn't shoot a dried pea two meters with that barrel if your name were Louis Armstrong."

The young man was breathing somewhat heavily. "You don't know it's not a gun. How do you know it's not a gun?"

" 'Cause I didn't leave a gun for you to find on the path. I left you a piece of pipe to find."

"You left it for me to find?"

"Oh, yes. And then made the light from the study window shine on it. Anything to instill confidence in the younger generation. Encourage family visitations."

The young man behind Fletch took three more fairly deep breaths. "You know I'm your son?"

"Not yet."

After a few seconds the pressure against Fletch's head stopped.

Fletch asked, "Seeing I'm sitting and you're standing behind me, and therefore have the advantage, I ask you, may I move, please?"

"To do what?"

"To look at you. I'm mildly curious."

"About what?"

"To see what Crystal hath wrought."

"Crystal," the young man's voice said.

"Your mother. Crystal. Crystal Faoni is your mother, isn't she?"

After a deep breath, the voice said, "Okay."

Fletch swiveled slowly around in his desk chair.

Simultaneously, the young man turned around to face the far wall.

At first Fletch saw only the back of a soaking wet, lean male in his early twenties. The back of his denim shirt had stitched on it FEDERAL PENITENTIARY/TOMASTON.

Fletch tisked. "You kids. You can't wear anything without some sort of an advertisement or a slogan

oℂₒₒℂₒₒℂₒ

on it. Wouldn't the usual beer logo or 'YALE' do just as well?"

The young man stuck the piece of pipe into the back pocket of his wet jeans.

With his foot, Fletch slid the metal wastebasket from under his desk.

Apparently identifying the noise accurately, the young man turned. With a quick grin and a glance at Fletch, he dropped the pipe into the basket.

"You have your mother's eyes," Fletch said.

"She says the rest of me is pure you."

"Poor you. Your boots are messing up the floor." Up to their high-top laces they were covered with mud, manure, bits of hay.

"I always heard that father types say things like that."

"Take 'em off. Right where you are." Fletch tapped his foot against the side of the wastebasket. "You're not in a jailhouse now. No free labor here."

Standing on one foot, then the other, the young man removed one boot, filthy, wet white sock, dropped them in the wastebasket, then the other boot and sock. He asked, "Couldn't you say 'Hello' first? 'How are you? How's your life been?' "

"You like tuna puffs?"

"What's a tuna puff?"

"I liked them, your age. Still do. Warm food."

"I like warm food."

Passing between the young man and the desk, Fletch went into the study bathroom. He returned with two towels. One he handed to the young man. The other he dropped on the mess the young man's boots had made on the wood floor. He stirred the towel around with his foot.

"What's your name?" Fletch asked.

"John."

"Faoni."

"John Fletcher Faoni."

"True?"

"Too true."

"What do people call you?"

"Jack."

"Oh."

"Sometimes I say my name is Fletch."

"Oh. That sounds more familiar."

"Fletch Faoni. Lots of people are called Jack."

"Gee. And all this time I thought Crystal liked my first names."

"Irwin Maurice," Jack blurted.

Crouching on bent knees, Fletch finished cleaning up the mess on the floor. He picked up the towel and turned it over. "Would you believe I didn't know you exist?"

"I know you didn't. Mother didn't want you to."

Fletch looked up at the barefoot boy with cheeks wet with rain. Without using the towel, Jack had just hung it around his neck. "Why not?"

"Said I was none of your business. Shouldn't be a burden to you. You didn't ask for me. She conned you, entrapped you, or something. Way she tells it, she virtually had me by artificial insemination."

"Not quite. Although I think she would have had you by parthenogenesis, if she could have."

Jack did not ask what *parthenogenesis* meant.

Still crouching, wet, filthy towel in hand, Fletch continued to look up at the young man, who had not moved back, or away, across the room, who

o◯∘∘◯∘∘◯∘o

remained standing closer to Fletch than normal, as if to *sense* him.

Jack's hair was curled with rain and mud. His face was streaked by dirt in dried sweat, especially in his two-day-old light beard.

He smelled of outdoors, rain, sweat, trees, hay, exertion.

Fletch said, "We made love only once."

"She's told me you were both naked on a bathroom floor struggling to free yourselves from a shower curtain you had fallen through, or some such ridiculous thing. And so I got born."

"That's about right." Fletch smiled. "Entrapped in a shower curtain. Something like that. But she didn't exactly *entrap* me. We were at a journalism convention at Hendricks' Plantation, in Virginia. In fact, if I remember correctly, I entered the shower voluntarily. Of course, it was my shower, and I can't remember how she happened to be in it. What's more, it was a real case of coitus interruptus. I mean, after being interrupted by a third person, we both did return our attentions back to what apparently turned out to be your conception. She must have timed the occasion perfectly. It wasn't until later that I realized Crystal was trying to get pregnant. By me. Crystal always was good at timing things."

"How did you feel about that?"

"I was complimented."

"Did you love her at all?"

"Oh yes. Crystal was charming, brilliant, witty, thoughtful, perceptive, loving, with gorgeous skin and eyes. She could have been a great beauty."

o⬤ooⵊ⬤ooⵊⵔo

"Except she probably weighed a ton and a half."

"She felt she had a weight problem, yes. Does she still?"

"She weighs about right," Jack said, "if only she were fourteen feet tall."

"I think she hadn't many lovers."

"From what she'd told me," Jack said, "Mother made love only twice in her life. Once to you, and once, long before, to a man named Shapiro."

"Oh, yes. I remember now. That's how I figured out what she was doing. She had attempted this selective breeding once before."

"And was she terribly fat even then?"

"Corpulent." Fletch dumped the dirty wet towel into the wastebasket. He stood up. "Trouble with Crystal was that she thought she was unattractive. She told everybody she was unattractive all the time. So most people saw her as unattractive."

Jack said, "You did what you did without forethought."

"You're well-spoken. Yes. Without much forethought. But I could have done something else."

"I'm glad you didn't."

Fletch cut his eyes to read the young man's face. "Are you?"

"Oh, yes."

"Did I make a mistake?"

Finally the young man stepped into the middle of the room. His eyes scanned the light switches. "Do the lights in this house go on automatically?"

"Why do you ask?"

"Because the lights went on one by one. Fifteen minutes later you came down the road in the Jeep

o◯ooo◯ooo◯o

by yourself. What do you have, some kind of a radio switch in the Jeep?"

Fletch asked, "In which barn are your traveling companions?"

The young man hesitated. "The one further from here."

"Do they smoke? Do they have matches, lighters?"

"They don't smoke. I don't know if they have lighters."

"If they have matches they're probably soaked and useless."

"How did you know about them? My 'traveling companions'? Why do you call them that?"

"I met the sheriff on the way home. There are roadblocks up. They're looking for you."

"Oh. And the sheriff mentioned the name Faoni to you?"

"Kriegel. Faoni. Leary. Moreno. Which one are you?"

"What do you mean?"

"The murderer, the attempted murderer, the kidnapper, or the drug grocer?"

"Attempted murder."

"I see."

The young man stood very straight. "I'm asking you if you are alone in the house. I know there was no one in the house before you arrived."

"You're trying to tell me you've got big, tough friends outside."

"Yeah."

Fletch moved some of the papers on his desk, revealing the handgun. He picked it up and put it in his belt. "You saw me arrive alone."

The young man raised his chin a little. Still he seemed to be sniffing Fletch warily. "Yes."

"The barns are the first places the cops will look for you, and your traveling companions. As kids they hid in barns themselves." Jack said nothing. Pointing, Fletch said, "Uphill of the back barn, to the left, about one hundred and fifty meters, is a deep gully. There's all kind of junk, trees, old barbed wire, fence posts, whatever, thrown in that gully as somebody's idea of a means to prevent erosion. In a storm like this, shortly, if not already, water will come streaming hard down that gully. I'm certain the cops will not go into that gully." *They will not go into that gully,* Fletch knew, *because as kids they learned that's one of the places where the snakes are.* He asked Jack, "Do you want to help your traveling companions escape?"

Jack said, "Yes."

"Then go lead them up to the gully, tell them to hunker down in it, and to stay there until further notice." *Further notice will come,* Fletch continued in his own mind, *after your traveling companions have been thoroughly exhausted, terrified by snakes, and beaten up by rushing water beating them against trees, fence posts, and coils of rusty barbed wire.* "Better put your boots back on. Outside."

"Why are you helping me? I, we're a danger to you. And you'd better believe it."

"Hey. Aren't fathers supposed to grab every minute they can get to spend with their sons? I mean, here you are, taking probably just a short vacation from a federal penitentiary; clearly you've gone considerably out of your way to come see your old dad . . . "

Narrowing his eyes slightly, Jack said, "You're 'mildly curious' about me."

"Sure I am. What with the cops looking high and low for you, we'll have some real quality time together. Don't you think?"

"You're not sending me out to hunker down in a gully with the other guys?"

Fletch said, "There's a shower in there." He nodded to the door to the study bathroom. "Fresh towels. Down the hall, back of the house, there's a guest room. Closets, bureau drawers. Some old clothes of mine; some left by forgetful houseguests. While you're showering and changing, I'll go heat up the tuna puffs. You want milk?"

"We knocked out your phones. Way down the road."

Fletch shrugged. "Some people around here still believe that when it rains real hard like this frogs drop out of the sky. When it rains this hard, there certainly are a great many more frogs on the roads. I've noticed that myself."

"What are you talking about?"

"When I come back, try to look more like a prince, will you? A little less like a frog?"

The young man tried to smile, but failed. "Why?"

"A couple of counties are about to stop by. They want to borrow the Jeep to go looking for you and your traveling companions."

"What are counties?"

From the hall outside the study, Fletch said: "Cops."

o❮○○○❮○○○❯o

chapter 3

Pulling off his sneakers as he walked, Fletch went through the kitchen into the small back hall. He stepped into his thigh-high black rubber boots. From a wall peg, he took his wide-brimmed dark brown hat and put it on his head. He buttoned his long, brown horse coat to his throat.

Knowing himself virtually invisible and inaudible in the night's hard rain, he went out the back door, and along the side of the house to the front corner.

Outside the French doors, Jack was visible in the study lights, sockless, stamping on his work boots. He crouched to lace them.

As Fletch knew he would, Jack went down the front walk, across the road, and along the graveled driveway through the home pasture to the barns.

After waiting a moment, Fletch crossed the lawn, the road, and went in a straight line over a white board fence, across the home pasture to the back fence. He sat on the top board of that fence under a tree. From there, even in that rain, even in that dark, he could see movement in the area between the barns and against the back hills. Fletch had learned that if he remained perfectly still, especially sitting, especially if he lowered his head so that his hat was backed by his shoulders, he would not be seen under such circumstances, or at least not be seen as a human.

In a moment a skinny man walked, head down, between the barns. He was headed in the direction of the gully. He took rapid short steps.

There followed a huge man, with a big egg of a head, big chest, big gut. Angrily he was waving his arms. More visible once backed by the hill, he turned. Shouting something, he ran back a couple of meters.

Suddenly, smoothly, a tall, slim, lithe figure ran forward to him, and kicked him in the crotch. The lighter man, the boy, cracked the side of his right hand against the egg of the big man's head. The young man's voice came through the pounding rain. "Will you shut up!" Then the young man backed up a meter and postured himself defensively.

The fourth man, shorter than all of them, fatter, came into view. Arms akimbo, he stood over the crouching big man. Fletch guessed he was talking to him, exhorting him.

While he talked, the lithe young man Fletch knew

to be Jack jogged ahead of the first man Fletch had seen, who was hesitating by the gate to the pastures.

Jack climbed over the gate. He disappeared across the stream toward the back hill.

Stepping on every rung of the gate, the second man followed.

Angrily shaking the gate as he climbed it, the big man climbed over the gate.

As if puzzled by the problem of gate climbing, the fat, bandy-legged man watched him. He looked for a way of opening the gate, but in the dark did not succeed. Then, clumsily, making more of a job of it than necessary, he climbed over the gate.

Faoni, Moreno, Leary, and Kriegel disappeared across the roaring stream, stumbling and slipping uphill in the dousing rain.

"Hey, Ace."

"That you, Fletch?"

"Yes, ma'am."

"Alston just came in." It was two hours earlier by the clock in California. "Hang on."

Alston Chambers and Fletch went back a long way together.

Alston had started his career as a prosecutor. When his children were born he decided he needed to earn a better living than the state provided him.

He tried being a defense attorney. He did make more money.

He hated defending people he knew to be criminals.

"The difference is," he told Fletch at the time,

"between telling the truth and distorting truth, making up a barely palatable lie to fit the facts, to seed reasonable doubt."

"Not your bowl of minestrone, eh?"

"I hate my clients! I think most of them should be hung, drawn, and quartered. How can I spend my life hating the people I work with, spend all my time with, my clients?"

"Many do."

"It's like being a beautician in the land of the ugly!"

"There's always divorce law," Fletch said. "Personally, I can tell you how profitable that is."

"I want to put all my clients in prison!"

"Then go back to putting them in prison," Fletch said. "You were good at it."

So, after time, with periodic objective advice, encouragement, and a few legitimate political dollars from Fletch, Alston Chambers had risen to the position of District Attorney.

Alston came on the phone. "Can't you let me get home, let me take off my coat, smell the stew pot, and pat the cat before making me answer the phone?"

"You're late. You must have slowed and smirked going by the county jail again. Did any of the citizens you've jugged wave at you as you went by? I know how you love that."

"Are you in a factory?"

"No. Why?"

"What's that noise?"

"Rain on an aluminum roof. Hard rain. I'm in the smokehouse."

"Why? Are you going to talk dirty to me?"

∘◌∘∞◌∞◌∘

"Probably." Fletch had taken the cellular phone from the station wagon into the smokehouse. Frequently, the phone did not work in the deep valley of the farm. Despite the storm, the phone was working well. Through the open door of the unlit smokehouse he could keep his eye on much of the farm. Probably he would be able to see Jack returning to the house, his dark shape moving along the white board fence. Hoping the phone would not leak, especially that his conversation would not be heard on some police frequency, he had finger-punched out Alston's home number in California.

"Hey, Alston," Fletch said. "Listen."

"Never mind. Take your time," Alston said. "We're just having duck curaçao for dinner. Those little onions."

"I have a son."

For a moment, Fletch thought the line went dead. It hadn't.

"I suppose you do," Alston said. "I never thought about it. A new son, or an old son?"

"An old son."

"How old?"

"You remember Crystal Faoni?"

"I remember your talking about her. That was two million years ago."

"Two and a half."

"You were never romantically involved with Crystal whatever-is-her-name. Were you? She's the one female in your life I thought you weren't romantically involved with."

"She had a son and never told me."

"How did she do that? Just by standing close to

o◯oo◯oo◯o

you? Did she catch your fumes or something?"

"We bumped into each other. Once."

"Wasn't she impossibly obese?"

"Corpulent."

"You could reach?"

"Apparently."

"Good for you. As I remember, you loved her mind, her wit, her good spirits . . . "

"I guess she saw something in me, too."

"What?"

"God knows."

"You mean, she wanted a kid by you? She set you up?"

"I could have resisted."

"Not you."

"I acted without forethought."

"What, did she sneak into your bed one night when you were half drunk, or something?"

"She tumbled out of my shower. Actually, she landed on me."

"Ah," Alston said. "The oppressed male."

"I've wondered why I haven't heard from her in years."

"Legally—"

"I don't care about legally."

"You never do. Where is this scion of sin?"

"Here."

"Where?"

"At the farm."

"And he's locked you in the smokehouse in the pouring rain?"

"Not quite."

"What does he look like?"

"I haven't really seen him yet. He's so dirty—"

"You mean 'dirty' as in so dirty you can't even see what he looks like?"

"He came through this storm," Fletch said, "under adverse circumstances. Over hill and dale, as it were. Through woods and streams."

"Does he have a brain?"

Fletch considered. "I think he knows what *parthenogenesis* means."

"Tell me what it means."

"It means a world without lawyers."

"Fletch, is this kid making some claims upon you?"

"I don't know his intentions."

"Because, besides checking such things as dates, if you can remember, if you have any records, there are such things as DNA tests—"

"I don't think there's much doubt about it. Crystal wasn't exactly the town pump."

"I suppose not."

"I remember realizing, belatedly, that Crystal probably had done this on purpose."

"Used you as stud."

"Ah . . . We only came together in this way once, Alston."

"Some guys have all the luck. Now that I think about it, I wonder just how many kids you do have. Probably half the younger generation are your brats. God, they all act like you. As soon as I figure out where they are, and what they're thinkin' and doin', damn-all if they're not thinkin' and doin' somethin' else."

"Be nice."

oᴑᴑᴑᴑᴑᴑᴑᴑo

"Why?"

"Because I'm about to ask you for two favors. The situation here is a little difficult."

"Reheated roast duck is never as good," Alston said.

"The house phones are dead. I'm making this call on the cellular phone on the sly, you see."

"In the smokehouse. In the pouring rain. You mean the kid hasn't really locked you out of your house yet?"

"I can't make many calls. Any other calls, for right now. I'm depending upon you, Alston."

"For what?"

"To find out where Crystal is. Her last name is spelled F-A-O-N-I."

"You want to send flowers? A little late."

"Address. Phone number."

"Can't you get that from the kid?"

"Will you do it for me, please?"

"After I don't let this duck go to waste. You know she never married?"

"I infer she hasn't."

"Where was she the last time you knew where she was?"

"Boston."

"When was that?"

"Twenty years ago. Twenty years plus."

"Great. By now she could be a man named McGillicuddy."

"Also, there was a jailbreak, earlier today, last night, yesterday. From the federal prison in Tomaston, Kentucky."

"That's not too far from you."

o◯oo◯oo◯o

"Not too far. Four escapees."

"What do you want to know?"

"Everything."

"Know anything at all about them?"

"Their crimes. Murder, attempted murder, kid-napping, and drug violations of some sort."

"Sweethearts."

"I know their names."

"But you're not going to tell me. What is this, some kind of a pass/fail test?"

"Leary, Moreno, and Kriegel."

"That's three."

"John Fletcher Faoni."

"What?"

"Spelled F-A-O-N-I."

"Jesus Christ. You poor sod. To think a moment ago I was envying you. You discover you have a son . . . a big bundle of joy . . . an escapee from the federal pen . . . a convicted—what?"

"He says attempted murder is his particular indis-cretion."

"Attempted murderer."

" 'The Truth is not for us to know, just now . . .' " Fletch quoted. " 'So are the mysteries well found-ed.' "

"Fletch, are these guys around your place now? Are they all there? Where's Carrie?"

"Upstairs. In bed. Sleeping peacefully."

"I know the Attorney General of—"

"Please, Alston, just make the calls I asked you to make. Cops are here, too. Sort of. This just happens to be a rather big band I'm trying to conduct at this moment. Too much bass, maybe."

"Yeah. Rather heavy in the rhythm section, too. I can feel it in my ears from here. Shit, my blood pleasure. I mean, pressure. Look what you're doin' to me! You're on that godforsaken farm, a million miles from who cares, in a raging storm, crawlin' with escapees from a federal penitentiary, real hard-timers, Carrie snoring in her bed—"

"Carrie doesn't snore. She wouldn't. She's the quietest damned sleeper—"

"Your phones are off. Did these guys cut the lines?"

"Yes."

"Next time I ask you why you're calling me from the smokehouse in the pouring rain, will you give me a straight answer?"

"I did. You just needed a little background." Fletch did see Jack moving, head down, along this side of the home pasture fence toward the front of the house. "I believe one of these guys is my son, Alston. I believe he led these other guys out of their way to come here. I want to know why. Okay? So please just do as I ask. And don't try to call me. You'll just add timpani to the bass. I'll call you back when I can. Enjoy your duck."

"Yeah," Alston said. "Duck you."

"Hey, Mister Fletcher." Deputy Sheriff Will Sanborne leaned his wet head and shoulders through the back doorway of the house. His feet were still in the mud outside.

"Hey, Will." In the kitchen, Fletch was filling two mugs with coffee. "You look wetter'n the minute you were born."

o❍∞❍o❍∞o

"Who's that guy movin' around in your library?"

"There's no guy in my library."

"A kid."

"Oh, you mean Jack? You want cream or sugar?"

"Black, please."

"That's my son, Jack."

Leaning from outside into the back hallway, Will wrinkled his face. "Your son, Jack?"

"You never met Jack?"

"Never knew you had a son."

"You didn't? Well, I'll be a hoppy toad. I thought everybody knew my son, Jack. Who's with you?"

"Michael."

"Come on in, Michael."

"Where's Carrie?"

"Upstairs in bed."

"Anyone else here?"

Fletch handed Will the hot coffee at the back door. "So you guys cased the place before entering. Pretty smart. I appreciate it. Come in."

"We'll mess up your floor."

"It's brick. Cleans easy."

In the small, dark back hall the two deputies looked very large in their slickers and hats. Leaving their slickers on, they put their wet hats on the wall pegs. Removing their boots together in that small space, they looked like two bears having their first dancing lesson.

"Oops." Will spilled some of his coffee on the floor.

In gray hunting socks they stepped into the kitchen.

Fletch handed Michael a mug of coffee.

"Thanks."

o◯oo◯oo◯o

"You're here for the Jeep," Fletch said.

"Yeah." Will blew on his hot coffee before sipping it. "Sheriff said to run it over your place first."

"These guys are here somewhere," Michael said. "For sure."

"The wet grass will be right slippery," Fletch said. "Don't try too tight a turn in that Jeep, especially in four-wheel drive, especially if you've got any speed up. Don't get yourselves in too great an angle on the hillsides."

Michael said, "You sound like my father." At twenty-one, Michael had just been released from the Army. He had hoped for a twenty-year career, as his father had had.

"Is that bad?" Fletch asked.

Michael said, "No." Then he laughed into his coffee cup. "Give me a break."

"You might check the barns," Fletch said.

Will said, "We'll check the barns."

Both had six-battery, head-cracking flashlights sticking out of their slickers' pockets.

Will stared at the .38 in the waistband of Fletch's jeans.

"There are four of these guys?" Fletch asked.

"Three," Michael said.

"Three? The sheriff said four."

Michael shrugged. "Maybe."

"When did they escape?"

"Sometime during the night," Will answered. "Probably early last night."

"Anybody hurt?"

"I don't think so."

"How did they get out?"

o☾o○○☾○○☽o

"Don't know," Will answered. "It's a maximum-security prison, isn't it?" he asked Michael.

"I thought so. These guys are murderers."

"Yeah." Frowning, Will looked into his coffee cup. "We've been told to shoot on sight."

"Sorry," Fletch said. "Protect yourselves."

Will said, "Sheriff told us to check every room in your house, Mister Fletcher. I guess even the room where Ms. Carrie's asleep." He looked at Fletch's handgun again. "Idea is, they could have Ms. Carrie hostage in one room while you're sweet-talkin' us."

"Me? Sweet-talk anybody?" Fletch grinned. "I understand."

"One of us will stay downstairs while the other goes upstairs with you." Will rinsed his empty coffee mug in the sink.

"Sure."

"Last time I was here"—Will looked around—"we were all watchin' Atlanta play San Francisco on your big screen."

"I've never been here," Michael said. "You got any of those Tharp paintings, Mister Fletcher?"

"No. I guess I ran the price of them up too high for me to afford 'em."

"Sheriff ate two full-sized pizzas while watchin' the game," Will said. "Supremes. Never thought anybody could do that."

"He was nervous," Fletch said. "He bet on San Francisco."

Michael put mock horror on his face. "You guys were gamblin'?"

"It's all right, Michael," Fletch said. "It was rigged. Carrie was working the odds. You know how diplomatic she is. The sheriff was the only one who lost."

"He made up for it in the pizza he ate," Will said.

Turning on and off lights again, Fletch led them from room to room on the ground floor. The deputies checked closets, bathrooms.

Fletch heard the sounds of a guitar being tuned.

They came to the study.

Under the bright lights of the study's chandelier, on the big, blue, leather divan, sat John Fletcher Faoni.

His hair was dry and combed. He was clean shaven.

He was as clean as a fresh bar of soap.

Barefoot, he wore shorts and a T-shirt.

He was suntanned.

He looked up from the acoustic guitar he was tuning.

To the deputies following Fletch into the study, looking up, smiling, Jack said, "Ha!"

"I'll be damned," Fletch said. "You clean up pretty good, for a frog. Just maybe pigs can fly." Louder, he said, "This is my son, Jack Fletcher. Deputies Will Sanborne and Michael Jackson, Jack."

Putting aside the guitar, Jack stood and shook hands with the deputies. "How're you guys doin'?" Jack asked.

"Oh, my God," Fletch muttered. "A Southern prince yet."

"How come I don't know you?" Michael asked. "We're the same age."

"Didn't go to school here," Jack answered.

"I don't know you either," Will said. "I've never seen you around."

o❍∞❍∞❍o

Jack hitched up his shorts slightly. "That's because my daddy's just a little bit ashamed of me." At the word *daddy* Fletch felt like an electric shock hit his lower spine. "He took exception to my being born plumb ignorant and kept me away from him all my growin' up years in one school after another."

"He was raised by his mother," Fletch said.

"Still—" Michael said.

"Who's your mama?" Will's question wasn't as suspicious as it was country curious. The next question, with any pretext, would be, *She got kin around here?*

"Her name's Crystal," Jack said. "She's in the radio business up north."

Jack had eliminated the pretext. His mother was a Yankee. Named Crystal.

"She's a career woman," Fletch said.

Will said to Fletch, "His mama got custody of him?"

Fletch said, "Yeah."

Will shook his head sadly. Fletch remembered Will had lost custody of his two children in a divorce. His wife had claimed that because of his hours, because of the danger of his job, because he wore a gun, Will was not as appropriate a parent as she.

"How long are you goin' to be here?" Michael asked. "You get a license, I'll show you where some of the best fishin' holes are."

"I'm driving him down to the University of North Alabama in the morning," Fletch said.

Jack threw a glance at him.

"Good," Michael said. "You'll be home some weekends. We'll work something out. Call me when you

◦◯◦◦◯◦◦◯◦◦◯◦

know you're comin' home. Your daddy knows my daddy." He looked at Jack's narrow waist, flat stomach. "You drink beer?"

"Do fish like water?"

"What kind of beer you like?"

"The wet, cold kind." Jack laughed.

Michael shook Jack's hand again. "We'll work somethin' out."

"I'll stay downstairs," Will said, "while you two check out the rooms upstairs."

Michael said to Jack, "There are some escaped convicts around here."

"I know." Jack laughed. "At first I thought Daddy got the pistol out 'cause my head was spendin' too much time in the refrigerator."

"He just arrived," Fletch said. "Hungry."

Leading Michael up the stairs, Fletch heard Will, in the study, say to Jack, "I never even noticed a picture of you in this house."

Jack said, "Well, my mama and my daddy haven't had anything to do with each other for a long time now. One of those things. She needed my loyalty, you know?"

Fletch waited in the front hall upstairs while Michael checked the attics, the snuggery, the other bedroom.

"Ms. Carrie in there?" Michael whispered.

"Yes."

"I'll just crack open the door." He leaned into the master bedroom. After he closed the door, he grinned. "Is she dead?"

"She sleeps quietly."

"Does she stop breathing?"

o◠ooᗧooᗤo

"She doesn't work at it."

When they went downstairs, Will asked, "Every-thing okay?"

"Right as a whiff of magnolia on a summer's breeze," Michael said.

Jack shook hands with both deputies again. "Hap-py hunting," he said cheerily.

Fletch led the deputies back to the kitchen.

As they were putting on their boots, Will said, "Now, Mister Fletcher. If they're on the farm and watching, they know we've been here. As we patrol the farm, we just might squeeze them into the house. You know what I mean?"

"Yes."

"You all are probably in more danger now than if we were never here."

"I understand."

Michael opened the back door. It was still raining hard.

"Don't you hesitate to use that pistol."

Fletch thought of the charming, healthy, beautiful young man in his study. His son? "I won't."

"Thanks for the coffee," Michael said.

"You all come back," Fletch said. "You hear?"

o◖○oo◖○oo◖○o

chapter 4

"Nice place you have here." Jack cleared the coffee table of albums when he saw Fletch enter with a tray. "I could have come to the kitchen. Or wherever."

Fletch put the tray on the coffee table. On the tray were the warm tuna fish sandwiches, a glass, and a half gallon of milk.

"I frequently eat in here."

"How old is it?"

"The tuna fish? Probably ten, twelve years old."

"The house."

"Antebellum."

"Here that means before the Civil War, not the Revolutionary War, that right?"

"The Brothers' War," Fletch said. "The War

Between the States." He sat in a wing chair. "You should know. You just oozed Southern like someone running for the office of county dogcatcher."

"Not really." Jack was nearly inhaling his sandwiches and milk. "Just tryin' to be nice to your friends." Jack grinned. "His daddy knows my daddy."

The electric shock to Fletch's lower spine at Jack's use of the word *daddy* was just as strong this time.

"So tell me," Fletch asked, "whom did you attempt to murder?"

"A cop."

"Oh, God!"

"No. A cop."

"Son of a bitch."

"That's no way to speak of Crystal."

"It's a wonder you're still walking around."

"I didn't actually kill her."

"A lady cop?"

"I didn't stop to ask."

"You just *tried* to kill her."

"I tried."

"And what was your doubtlessly magnificent reason for this criminal behavior?"

"She was bothering a friend of mine."

"Where was this?"

"Louisville, Kentucky."

"What were you doing in Louisville, Kentucky?"

"Heading south."

"Where south? Here?"

"Maybe. Nashville, anyway."

Fletch looked at the guitar Jack had found in the guest bedroom. It had been a house present from a

o◖ooᏅooᏅo

country music star who had needed to stay at the farm awhile. It had the star's name on it. Since it had been left, no one had played it. The guitar had become an ornament, a prized, dusted ornament. "Are you musical?"

Jack shrugged. "We wanted to find that out."

"Who's 'we'?"

"My friend and I. He plays keyboard."

"Where is he now?"

"Kentucky state pen."

"And how and why was this woman cop bothering your friend?"

"It had to do with the car he was driving."

"What about it?"

"It was stolen." Jack smiled. "A pink Cadillac convertible. Vintage."

"Wonderful." Fletch shook his head. "You wanted your pink Cadillac convertible before you even got to Nashville."

"Something like that. Arriving in style."

"Some style. So what happened?"

"I shot at her. Just to discourage her from making the arrest. Arresting my friend. I didn't need to do anything. I wasn't even in the car at the moment. I could have disappeared, gotten away, saved my own ass. I didn't realize other cops had snuck up behind me. They hit me over the head. Bastards. I was convicted of the attempted murder of a police officer. Would you believe that?"

"Yes."

"People don't appreciate loyalty."

"Police officers have every reason to discourage such behavior."

∘☾∘∘∘☾∘∘∘☾∘

"Sure. Still, it just happened. In the heat of the moment. You had to have been there."

"No, thanks. You shot at her with what?"

"A pistol. A .32."

"Why would you even have such a thing?"

"We had it. You know, traveling. We intended to sleep out at night."

"You weren't in the car, but you had the gun on you."

"I had put it under my shirt. I was going into a store."

"Did you intend to rob the store?"

"No. Who'd try to rob a supermarket?"

"Then why were you carrying the gun?"

"It felt good against my skin."

"You have trouble getting it up, son?"

Jack's eyebrows raised. "No."

"I don't see why you were carrying the gun."

Jack said, "You've got a gun stuck into your jeans. Right now."

"By order of the sheriff." Fletch got up and went to the open French doors. "I'm surrounded by fugitives from justice. A least one of them, of you all, is a murderer." He had his back to Jack. "You're all murderers, come to think of it. Kidnapping, drugs: you've all taken big holes out of people's lives. In this life, who are the bastards?"

Jack muttered, "The fathers, or the sons?"

From the window, through the rain, Fletch saw the headlights of the Jeep high on the hill, well above the gully. One of the big flashlights was piercing the dark from the passenger side of the vehicle.

"Aren't you afraid to stand in the lit window?"

Jack asked. "Under the circumstances?"

"No." Fletch turned his back to the window.

Knees apart, arms at his sides, Jack was slouched on the divan.

Fletch said, "You have your mother's skin."

"Not all of it." Jack stretched his arms. "By a dam's site."

"How come you're tanned?" Fletch asked. "How long have you been in prison?"

"Five weeks. Before that I was out on bail. Just hanging around. Can't get much of a day job when you're out on bail on charges of attempted murder."

"Why didn't you come here?"

"Didn't want to bother you. Besides, I wasn't supposed to leave Kentucky, State of."

"You escaped from a maximum-security federal penitentiary after only five weeks?"

"I didn't like it there," Jack said. "Noisy. Food could have been better. I'd read all the books in the library."

"You know karate?"

"A type of." Again, Jack looked at Fletch in surprise. "Ah! You were outside, weren't you? You watched me lead my 'traveling companions' to the gully."

"What's the name of the big one you disciplined with your foot and the side of your hand?"

"Leary. He's crazy."

"And which is Kriegel?"

"The short, bald guy, with eyeglasses. His name is Kris Kriegel, with a K. Would you believe that? How did you follow me?" Jack looked at Fletch's sneakers, the cuffs of his jeans. "You're not wet."

oᴄ◯ooᴄ◯oo◯o

In a more conversational tone, Fletch asked, "Where is Crystal?"

"Generally, or at the moment?"

"Generally. And at the moment."

"Indiana."

"Is she working as a journalist?"

"Sort of. No." Jack sat forward. "She owns five radio stations."

"Good for her."

"She calls them her money machines. We live, lived outside Bloomington." He poured himself more milk. "At the moment, she's on her semiannual sojourn on a fat farm. She locks herself up for two weeks twice a year. *Incommunicado.* Concentrates on losing weight. She has to. If she doesn't, she can't walk . . . " Fletch saw an exasperation based on love in Jack's face. "Her legs will crack under her. Her veins . . . her heart . . . "

Jack had eaten every bit of food from the tray.

"You want more food?" Fletch asked.

Quickly, Jack sat back. "No. No, thanks. Maybe later."

Fletch sat at the desk. "How did you know where I live?"

"We see your name in the newspapers once in a while. Ever since you wrote the book *Pinto: The Biography of Edgar Arthur Tharp, Junior.* That was a big success, wasn't it?"

Fletch asked. "Did you read it?"

"Yeah."

Fletch waited for Jack to say more. After a moment of silence, Fletch said, "I guess it's been praised enough."

∘●∘∘●∘∘●∘

"Big book," Jack said.

Fletch said, "It took a while."

Jack took a deep breath. "Where do you get off writing a book concerning Native Americans—*Indians*—white man?"

Fletch said, "Where did Edgar Arthur Tharp, Junior, get off painting Native Americans—*Indians*—sculpting them? He was a 'white man,' too."

"Exactly. He painted and sculpted them as part of their horses. You said so yourself. In your book. You wrote, 'Tharp stretched and lit the naked muscles of the Indian riders exactly as he did the muscles of the horses on which they rode.' Right?"

"Right."

" 'He painted the women, rounded, with babies on their backs, in the same configurations as the earth mounds behind them.' "

"So," Fletch said. "You read the book."

"I read the book."

"You giving me an argument about my work?"

"I'm giving you an argument."

"Okay." Fletch sighed. "Where did a Harvard-educated, Jewish American male get off writing, composing *West Side Story* about urban Puerto Rican youngsters, based on a play about youngsters in Verona, Italy, called *Romeo and Juliet* written by a white, male Englishman named William Shakespeare, who had never been to Italy?"

Jack grinned. "I guess you're familiar with this argument."

"Yeah. I've confronted it, once or twice. I have been surprised to perceive the prejudice against my work, in one or two quarters."

o❍○○◯○○◯o

"What's the answer?"

"In the first place, it never occurred to me. I know what I am. And I know what I am not. At least unlike some, I know I cannot *be* someone else, truly see and feel from someone else's experience and heart. Nevertheless, I have always believed in empathy, in the broad commonality of being human. Admittedly, we cannot understand. But we can try. Too, although Native Americans had and have a great art, Tharp's representation of them, and the cowboys, the steam locomotives, the horses, the buffalo, were representations the Indians and the settlers were not about to do themselves. Tharp memorialized them, with empathy and love. Without his works, we would know less, understand less. And I tried to memorialize Tharp and his works with empathy and love."

"You're lecturing."

"You asked a question. I answered it."

"You believe in straight lines, don't you?"

"Nature does not love the straight line," Fletch said. "Man is compelled to it."

" 'Man'?"

"Broadly speaking."

"Is that a pun?"

"I think I've just learned not to feed you."

Jack folded his arms across his chest. "My mother tried to write a book once. She only did about eighty pages. Half of it was about you. Half of it was about me. She loves to tell stories about you."

"She used to beat people over their heads with stories about me."

"Any of them true?"

"Not really."

oᴏＯoooＯoooＯo

"How about the time you were in Brazil and the people there took you for the ghost of someone murdered even before you were born, and you had no choice but to solve the murder of yourself?"

"Crystal told you that story?"

"What about it?"

"A ghost story."

"My mother loved you. She still does. She loved you sexually as well, you know."

"I guess I didn't understand that."

"You married a royal princess? I saw that in the newspapers, too."

"I was married to a princess, yes."

"She was murdered."

"Assassinated."

"Why?"

"Middle Europe. Politics. Ethnicity."

"Is ethnicity politics?"

"Oh, yes. In our coming together and our moving apart. Just politics. Always just a few people seeking power for themselves."

"Were you with her when . . . your wife . . . was assassinated?"

"I was in the car behind her. Annie Maggie never thought about politics. She thought about cooking. She thought about the various kinds of fruits, and cheeses, and sauces, new potatoes and cutlets."

"Was she fat?"

"No."

"And you're alone here now, on the farm?"

"I was going to apologize to you for all my questions," Fletch said.

"Oh, I knew you know how to ask questions."

o○Oooo○Oooo○o

"You were expecting my questions, weren't you?"

"You were a reporter."

"Aren't I still?"

Jack flicked a hand at the study's walls. "I don't know any reporter who lives this way. Why don't you have any paintings by Edgar Arthur Tharp?"

"Who can afford them? Besides, I spent years working on Tharp. One likes to think one can come to the end of something." He opened a desk drawer. He took out of it a pistol. From a separate, locked drawer, he took out the pistol's cartridge and a box of shells. "You know all this about me from newspapers and your mother, is that it?"

He crossed the study and put the pistol on Jack's lap. He placed the cartridge and the box of shells on the coffee table beside the tray.

Jack asked, "What's this?"

"A pistol," Fletch answered.

Jack sat up, with the pistol still on his shorts. "I know that. I mean, what are you doing?"

"Giving you a pistol."

"Why?" Besides having the pistol in his lap, Jack was touching no part of it. "Are you trying to trick me?"

"Would I do that?"

"Yes. I think so."

"You weren't with me in the Jeep when I came to that roadblock. Nor were you mentioned. An hour later, when the deputies arrived, you were here. How did you get here? Where's your vehicle? People here don't really, really believe frogs drop from the sky in a hard rain. The cops must have a description

of you. I want you armed. If the counties come back
knowing who you are, I want you to have the decen-
cy to tell them you have been holding me and—me
captive. Load it."

Jack put his hand into the box of shells. "You still
have your pistol."

"I can make it disappear faster than you can inhale
a tuna sandwich."

Jack concentrated on loading the cartridge.

Fletch said, "Aiding a fugitive from justice is
against the law."

"How about arming one?"

"You're not going to shoot anybody."

"Are you sure?"

"Positive."

Jack put only five shells into the cartridge. He put
the cartridge down.

"Load the cartridge into the gun," Fletch said.

Again watching himself carefully, Jack slid the
cartridge into the handgun's grip.

"Aren't you going to put a bullet into the chamber?" Fletch asked.

"Later." Jack placed the handgun on the divan
beside him.

The brass knocker on the front door banged more
than a half dozen times. Fletch smiled. He said:
"Hark."

He pulled his shirt out over the butt of the gun
in his waistband.

On the front porch stood a short, fat, balding man
in prison denims. From head to foot and side to side
he was covered with mud and manure. He squinted
through filthy, askew, steamed glasses.

"You're Kris Kriegel, the escaped murderer?"
Fletch asked.

"Yeah."

"Go around back."

Fletch slammed the door just as the man stepped
toward it.

Going back into the study, Fletch said to Jack,
"It's someone for you." The handgun he had given
Jack was not in sight. "I sent him around back. If
you can't keep the shit out of the house, at least
keep the mud out. Mud the cops will notice."

chapter 5

On the bed, Carrie was sitting on Fletch, still in the position in which both had climaxed.

"I could sit here forever," Carrie said, "feeling you inside me. What would you do if I sat here forever?"

On his back, Fletch shrugged. "Send out for Chinese, I guess."

Laughing, Carrie fell to her side on the rumpled bedsheets.

Climbing the stairs, Fletch had said to Jack, who was going along the hallway below him toward the back of the house, "I'm going to sleep."

He did not sleep.

He had rapped lightly on the bedroom door and

said, softly, "All escaped convicts are chickens."

When he inserted his head around the door frame into the dawn-lit room, Carrie's big, blue eyes were on high beam.

The shotgun was on the bed with her, aimed at the door. The index finger of her left hand was on the trigger.

Fletch laughed.

He closed the door behind him.

"Everything all right?" she asked.

"All things being relative."

Fletch took off his clothes and got onto the bed. "You're not ready to go downstairs yet, are you?" he asked.

"No."

She proved it.

Then, curled beside him, she asked, "Have we had any visitors?"

"Yeah. Santa Claus just showed up at the front door."

"Hate to tell you this, Yankee, but Santa doesn't come in the summertime." She giggled and punched Fletch in the ribs.

"Poor him. His name is Kris Kriegel. He's short, fat—"

Her head snapped back for a better look at Fletch's full face. "You're serious."

"Yeah. He's here."

"Who's here?"

"Kris Kriegel."

"One of the convicts! I thought I heard a pounding on the front door. It woke me up."

"Guess he couldn't find one of the chimneys. Two

oᴼᴼ◯ooᴼᴼᴼᴼᴼᴼ◯ooᴼᴼo

of the other convicts I guess are still hiding out in the gully."

"What gully? The big gully . . . ?" She moved her head to indicate direction. " . . . yonder?"

"Yeah."

"How do you know they're there?"

"I sent them there, to hide. Michael and Will came for the Jeep. They patrolled the place pretty well."

"The gully." Carrie made a face. "During the storm?"

"You care?"

"Why there? You knew that would turn into a ragin' flood. God, the snakes!"

"To wear them all out. If we're gonna have escaped felons around here, we might as well have exhausted ones."

"Have them around here! Why didn't you shoot them? Why didn't you turn them all in? You said Michael and Will were here." She sat up, cross-legged on the bed. Instantly, she was picking her fingers.

"Because of Jack."

"Who's Jack?"

"Carrie, I think he's my son."

Her head snapped to look at him.

He sat up, too. "I knew a woman, once, named Crystal Faoni. She was a journalist, too." Fletch spoke rapidly. "At a journalists' convention we made love, once. This boy's name is John Fletcher Faoni. He's one of the escaped convicts. Or, at least, he says that's his name. He seems to know about Crystal, about me."

"Faoni." She spoke slowly. "You recognized his

name last night, at the roadblock. That's why you began making sandwiches when you got home."

"It's not that common a name."

"Your *son!?* Why didn't you tell me?"

"I wasn't sure."

"I mean, why didn't you ever tell me you have a son?"

"I never knew he existed until he walked through the French doors of the study last night. Crystal is one of these women who wanted to have the baby, raise the child on her own. I believe that's true."

"She never let you know?"

"No."

"Are you upset about that?"

"Of course."

"How did you know he likes tuna puffs?"

Always Fletch was amazed at the acuity of Carrie's questions. Next to hers, District Attorney Alston Chambers's questions were vague. "Last night he would have eaten refried roadkill."

She put her hand on his forearm. "I'm sorry."

"Attempted murder," Fletch said. "He took a shot at a cop."

"$E=MC^2$!" Such was Carrie's expletive. She considered the theory of relativity the most *outlandish* thing she had ever heard of.

She looked out the window. "It's stopped raining."

"I think it will be a bright, hot day."

"The fields got a good wetting," she said.

"It flattened the corn."

"It will spring up again." She got up off the bed. "Why are you putting up with this? Even if he is, maybe, your son, he tried to kill someone; I mean, you have no responsibility for him. How old is he?"

"Curiosity."

"You know what curiosity did to the orangutan."

"What did curiosity do to the orangutan?"

"Go ask him. He's still sitting over in the Memphis Zoo. You saw how hellfire angry he still is."

"You heard the sheriff last night. For some reason, these escapees went well out of their way to come here, to this farm, this house, specifically. This kid, Jack, led them here. Why?"

Carrie said, simply: "To kill you."

"Why?"

"You're his father. You popped his mother and left her. You ignored him all his life."

"No," Fletch said. "He knows I never knew of his existence. The only thing is, well, I never called Crystal, an old friend, and said, *How're ya doin'*? That's not a capital crime."

"This is a crazy, mixed-up kid. He shot a cop."

"Shot *at* a cop. Supposedly."

She looked down at him. "What do you mean, 'supposedly'?"

"He said he fired a .32 at her. I just gave him my .32 to load. I watched him. It seemed to me he had to figure out how to load it. I don't think he knew how to chamber a bullet. He seemed to have a revulsion toward the gun."

"He should have," Carrie snapped. "What would you expect? And he shot at a woman cop?"

"Blue is blue," Fletch said. "I guess."

"You're making up excuses," she said. "You think he's your son, and you're trying to like him." She was reading Fletch's face. "You think this boy has anything but green water between his ears?"

Fletch thought of the conversation he and Jack had had about *Pinto*. "Enough to be a pest."

Forearms folded over her breasts, Carrie said, "These bastards. In this house!"

"There are still two outside. I guess I ought to go get them. Bring them in."

"Into this house?"

"This old house has been occupied by worse, I expect," Fletch said. "Yankees, probably."

Carrie was listening. "What's that? Someone playing the radio?"

"Someone playing the guitar."

"Who?"

"Jack."

"Jack!" she expostulated. "You call his name just as if he's someone you know."

"I'm getting to know him," Fletch said. "A little bit."

They listened to the acoustic guitar being played downstairs.

Carrie said, "He plays beautifully."

"So he does."

"Still," Carrie said, uncertainly. "I think you ought to call the sheriff and have them all picked up. Including your *Jack*. If he shot at a cop, he needs nothin' more than bein' put in a pit with fire ants." She was looking across the bed at the telephone.

"By the way," Fletch said. "The phones are dead. They cut the wires."

"I didn't think they came here to cook, clean, and paint fences. Does your cellular phone work?"

"Yes. But I don't want them to know I have it. I

o◖Ooo◖Ooo◖Oo

want to get these guys out of here before the telephone company discovers the wires have been cut. I told Will and Michael last night I'm driving Jack to the University of North Alabama this morning."

"They saw him? They met him?"

"They even talked with him. He was as smooth as a Mississippi River stone. Michael even invited him fishing."

"You passed him off as *your son?*"

"I sweet-talked 'em. A little."

"So you're stuck, aren't you. You're as stuck as the smile on a beauty queen's face."

"Except I gave Jack the .32. So he can hold us captive. If the cops come back."

"Say what?" Wide-eyed, she was looking down at him sitting cross-legged on the bed. "You done real good, Fletch. You've brought fugitive felons, murderers and such-like, into this house, and armed them! Against ourselves! Against the cops! When you came into this room, didn't I ask you if everything was all right?"

"And I said, *All things being relative.*"

"That was a joke?" In fact, Carrie did smile.

"Carrie, this kid wants something from me. How do I know what to believe? How do you know what to believe?"

"He wants you to save his ass."

"Maybe. I think it's worth stringing him along a little, extending myself, to find out what, why."

Picking her fingers, listening to the guitar, Carrie said, "You're always playing, Fletch. You still think you can handle anything. Everything."

"No. In fact, I don't. There are just things here

oOoooOoooOo

that don't add up. I want to know why."

Looking through the window again, Carrie said, "If we're gonna give these felons breakfast, we'll need the eggs from the henhouse."

"I'll get them!" Fletch sprang off the bed. "I allus obeys Ms. Carrie."

chapter 6

"Aha! Now I see!" Shiny clean, even unto his eyeglasses, his soft body encased in a guest bathrobe, Kriegel exclaimed when Fletch entered the study. The man had a saddle-shaped birthmark on the bridge of his nose. "Come here!" he said to Fletch grandly.

Fletch stayed where he was.

Behind Kriegel, Jack was standing stiffly.

Kriegel came to Fletch. With both hands, he fingered Fletch's head. He stood on tiptoes to do so. He walked around Fletch, looking him up and down. "You are Jack's father!"

"You're a phrenologist?" Fletch asked. He frowned at Jack.

"You have the same bones! The same blood!"

"You're a nut?" Fletch asked.

Turning, Kriegel went to Jack and clasped him by the shoulders. "This man is your father! Why didn't you tell me? He is one of us! We are saved!"

"Praise the Lord," Fletch said.

"Introduce me," Kriegel ordered Jack.

"Father," Jack said, standing at attention. "This is The Reverend Doctor Kris Kriegel!" For an instant, Jack put his hand to his mouth. "Doctor Kriegel, this is my father, Irwin Maurice Fletcher!"

Kriegel said, "I'm so pleased."

Fletch said, "Charmed, I'm sure."

Fletch saw that Kriegel, for all his role-playing as an emperor, or whatever, was fighting hard to stay awake. He was intoxicated with exhaustion. His arms and legs moved as if they were in water. Blinking, his eyelids spent longer closed than open. When not speaking, he breathed through his nose more in the rhythm of sleep than wakefulness.

Like a drunk pretending to be sober, Kriegel was only pretending to be awake, alert.

At the moment, he was no threat to anyone.

"Ah . . . " Kriegel was looking toward a curtain of one of the French doors. He staggered to it. "Poor butterfly!"

Fletch said, "That's a moth."

Gently, Kriegel cupped both hands over the moth on the curtain, capturing it. He brought it to the open French window.

With a grand gesture, he released the moth into the morning sky. "You're free! Fly away home, little butterfly."

oⓄoooⓄoooⓄo

"I suspect its 'home' is in my wardrobe," Fletch said.

"There is someone else in this house," Jack said sternly to Fletch. "I heard the bed jumping." He pointed to the ceiling. "You were right over this room."

"We heard you, too," Fletch said. "You play the guitar well. I recognized it as a Segovia arrangement of something, but I don't remember of what."

"Who is upstairs?" Jack asked.

"Nashville?" Fletch asked. "You were headed for Nashville in a pink Cadillac?"

Near the windows, Kriegel swayed, eyes closed.

"Your playing could charm a collicky baby covered with poison ivy," Fletch said.

Kriegel's eyes popped open when Carrie entered the study. He gasped. He raised his arms at his side. "Brunnehilde!"

"Broom Hilda?" In her tanned, freckled face, Carrie's wide-set blue eyes were flashing. Having ruled six large brothers, hefty farm workers, an ex-husband, sons, various obstreperous small children, and large animals, Carrie was the most dangerous person in that house, on the farm at that moment, Fletch reflected. Everyone might as well know it.

Having glanced contemptuously and dismissively at The Reverend Doctor Kris Kriegel, who looked like a dust ball in the gray robe, fuzzy gray hair sticking out over his ears, backlit against the French doors, she stared at Jack.

Jack returned the stare.

"Jack!" Kriegel said. "Is this your mother?"

Jack swallowed hard. "Of course not."

oⵔoooⵔoooⵔo

Carrie was considerably younger than Fletch, and looked even younger than she was.

Kriegel took a few steps toward Carrie and Fletch. It seemed his intent to take them by the hands.

Fletch stuck his hands in the pockets of his shorts.

Carrie turned her body square to him. Clearly, she was prepared to break his nose if he touched her.

"Brunnehilde and Siegfried!" Kriegel said. "How wonderful!"

"What's his engine revvin' for?" Carrie asked.

Fletch said, "I think we've caught a racist."

"$E=MC^2$!" She pointed her index finger at Kriegel. "You!" She pointed at the divan. "Go over there and lie down. You're half stupid tired. Your other half is probably just plain stupid." Shoulders drooping, Kriegel crossed the room to the divan. "And we don't want to hear no more of your stupid shit about Broom Hilda and what's-his-face. You hear?" Kriegel sat on the divan. He folded his hands in his lap. Smiling, he closed his eyes. She asked Fletch, "Who's what's-his-face?"

"Siegfried?"

"I never heard of nonesuch."

"Ask Wagner."

"Who's Wagner?"

"Wrote music."

"Got kinfolk around here?"

"Possibly."

Again, she was staring at Jack as she would a horse before saddling him. "Shit," she said. "He's your son, all right. Clear as a church bell on a crisp night. He's got your body."

"Oh, don't say that," Fletch said. "Last time someone said that about me and someone else, one of us got shot through a window."

"It wasn't you?" she asked.

"It wasn't me."

"I," Jack said. "It wasn't I, great writer."

Carrie pointed her finger in Jack's face. "And that's exactly enough sass out of you, you unbroke pony. You do any buckin' around here, and I'll personally whip your ass all the way back to that stable you come from in Kentucky. And you'd better believe it."

Jack's face couldn't be more startled if she had punched him hard.

He put his shoulders back. "Yes, ma'am."

Eyes closed on the couch, Kriegel chuckled. "Wonderful! I've found them!"

Quietly, smiling to himself, Fletch said, "You all better believe it."

"Ruinin' your life the way you done. Takin' a potshot at a woman just doin' her work. Handsome boy like you? The way you play that guitar? What's the matter with you anyway, boy?"

"Ah . . . " Clearly Jack had never been laced out by a Southern woman before.

Carrie continued, "What you doin' here anyway? Never got in touch with your father all the years of your growin' up, the minute you get in big trouble, runnin' from the law, you show up here in the middle of the night, draggin' these ugly messes behind you? What you want, boy?"

o☻ooᏅooᏅo

Jack glanced at Fletch. "Ah . . . "

She waved her hand at him. "I've heard and seen enough of you already. You guys go get some eggs." She looked at the obedient Kriegel asleep on the divan. "If that bag of manure moves one flap, I'll blast his parts all over the cornfield."

Fletch said to Jack: "She will. You'd better believe it."

Outside, Jack asked, "Eggs? How far is the store?"

Fletch ambled toward the barns.

Although the sun was just above the horizon, it already made steam rise from the puddles.

As he crossed the road, Fletch heard Emory's truck coming down the hill. That truck hadn't had a complete muffler in recent memory and could be heard well before being seen.

Jack walked beside Fletch.

"Who's she?" Jack asked.

"Carrie."

"You two married?"

"No."

"You going to get married?"

"These days you marry a woman and two lawyers. Beds just aren't that big."

Jack said, "She doesn't hesitate to rush in where fools would fear to tread, does she?"

Fletch said, "When Carrie twangs, you'd better listen."

Jack pointed across the home pasture at the cottage. "No one lives there. I checked last night."

"I can't figure out how you found this place so exactly yesterday," Fletch said. "Runnin' from the law. Through a storm. You've cruised this place before, haven't you? Scoped me out."

"Yes."

"As the man answered, when a friend told him he has passed his house the day before: Thanks." Most of the cattle on the hills were visible cropping the fields. Later, once the sun was higher in the sky, they would disappear in the deep shade of the trees. "What crime put your Kris Kriegel in jail?"

"When he first came from South Africa," Jack said, "in a hotel in Washington, the chambermaid, bringing in a mint for his pillow, or something, opened the door of his room just as he finished strangling a girl from some escort service. He was caught red-handed. Bare-assed and red-handed. Red-assed."

"How long has he been in prison?"

"Five, six years."

Fletch led Jack into the dark cool of the barn. "What's this 'The Reverend Doctor' stuff?"

"I believe he has a Ph.D. from someplace. A real one."

"Subject?"

"History, probably. Sociology? I don't know."

"And 'The Reverend' part?"

"I think he gave himself that while in prison. Sent five dollars for a certificate to someone advertising in the back of a magazine, or something."

At one of the barn's stalls, Fletch slipped the bit in Heathcliffe's mouth, the bridle and reins over his head. He fastened the buckle. "And what's your relationship to him?"

Jack said, "I'm his lieutenant."

"I see." Fletch led Heathcliffe out of the stall.

"Where are you going?" Jack asked. "How far is this store? Do you think you're getting away?"

"I'm going up the hill to get your two other traveling companions. Want to come? There's another horse there."

Jack was trying to stay close to Fletch but away from Heathcliffe. "They're too big."

"Not so big." Fletch climbed onto the horse. "Or you could jog along beside me."

"Don't you need a saddle?"

Fletch was riding through the back doorway of the barn into the corral. "Open that gate for me, will you?"

"Hey." Jack trotted behind the horse. "You're riding a horse barebacked in shorts."

"Yeah," Fletch said. "Just like a Native American."

Fletch sat on the horse at the lower end of the gully. Water still rushed down it noisily.

Sprawled in the gully, head down and forced into a loose bail of rusted barbed wire, left leg arced over an old washtub, was one of the escapees, the smaller, slimmer one, Moreno. His blank eyes stared at the cloudless sky of the new day. His throat was badly swollen.

Fletch guessed he had been bitten by either a rattlesnake or a copperhead, and then drowned.

Fletch said to himself, *And then there were three.*

From uphill came a loud, deep guttural noise. To Fletch it sounded like "Ou-row-ouu!"

o◯ooo◯oo◯o

He looked up to his right.

Charging down the edge of the gully toward him came Leary, all one-sixth of a ton of him. Soaking wet, muddy, he ran head down making this noise.

Fletch twitched Heathcliffe's rein, circled him around to the left.

As Leary pounded toward Fletch, Fletch rode the horse into him.

Leary fell back into the gully.

Fletch backed the horse off.

"Ow-row-ouu!" came from the gully.

Leary climbed out of the gully.

Again, bellowing, he charged Fletch.

Again Fletch rode the horse into him and sent Leary falling back into the gully.

The third time Leary climbed out of the gully, he stood on its edge a moment.

Fletch sat three meters away, watching him. He wondered if Leary might be thinking of a better way to solve his problems.

No. He was just catching his breath for a new charge.

"Ow-row-ouu!"

The fourth time Heathcliffe pushed Leary back into the gully, there was a god-awful holler.

"ARRRRRRRRR!"

After backing off, Fletch's feet flicked Heathcliffe forward to the edge.

In the gully, Leary had landed on Moreno's corpse. Arms and legs flailing, trying to get off the already bloating corpse, splashing in the rushing water, fighting off barbed wire, rotten fence posts, the holey washtub, Leary thrashed and bellowed until

oC)ooC)ooC)o

he was standing. Without hesitation he leapt at the side of the gully, flung himself against it. Kicking his legs, pulling with his arms, he scrambled up the gully's muddy side.

Standing again at the edge of the gully, Leary breathed hard. He looked down at the corpse now undulating deeper in the rushing water.

Fletch said, "Mornin'."

Leary's close-set eyes near the top of his egg-shaped head looked up at Fletch.

Fletch asked, "Are you hungry?"

Dry-heaving, clutching his stomach, Leary stumbled down the hills a meter in front of Fletch astride Heathcliffe.

Full lit by the low morning sunlight, Jack sat on the corral's fence watching them come over and down the last hill.

As they approached, he asked, "Where's Moreno?"

Herding Leary into the corral, Fletch answered, "Dead."

As Fletch rode Heathcliffe through the corral gate, Jack quoted, " ' . . . just the kind that kinsfolk can't abide . . . ' "

chapter 7

In the kitchen, Fletch said to Carrie: "Only three extra for breakfast."

"What happened to the other one?"

"Snakes got him."

Carrie didn't even look up from the stove. "Devil knows his own."

Fletch asked, "Ham? Country ham?"

"That's right," Carrie said with fierceness.

"It's going to be a right hot day," Fletch said.

"That's right," Carrie said in the same tone. "And I mean to give these bastards a case of thirst that'll make them unable to think of anything but cool, clear water. They'll just wish they could spit!"

"Well, don't give me any."

"Would I do that to you?"

"God knows what you'd do to a Yankee."

"Ah, Fletch. Don't think of yourself as a Yankee anymore. You're about gettin' over it."

Fletch began breaking eggs into a large bowl.

Jack had been amazed to see Fletch come out of the henhouse carrying eleven eggs. "Wow!" he said. "You make your own eggs!" Then he said, "They're dirty!"

Fletch said, "You think they were hatched already scrambled with milk and butter?"

Jack grinned. "I was hatched sunnyside up, I was."

"I see," Fletch said. "So you scrambled yourself."

Near them on the driveway outside the henhouse, Leary, clutching his stomach, stumbled around in small circles. Exhausted, bruised, frightened, nearly drowned, run over by a horse, terrified by landing on a corpse, he was about as worn down as a man could be.

Fletch thought Leary did not have a whole lot of fight left in him.

Emory had parked his noisy truck in the shade of one of the sheds. He had fed the horses and the hens.

When Fletch came out of the henhouse, Emory was standing aside. First his eyes studied Jack. Then Leary.

Then he looked at Fletch.

Fletch said, "Say hello to Jack Fletcher, Emory."

"Jack Fletcher?" It was hard to surprise or impress Emory. In the years Emory had worked for Fletch he had seen many people, country-music stars, authors, politicians, African and African-American leaders, slip on and off the farm. When people in the area asked Emory who had just been to the farm, Emory's answer had always been the same: *I didn't notice.* Fletch knew Emory would not ask if Jack were son, nephew, cousin, or coincidence.

Emory and Jack shook hands.

Warily, Emory looked at Leary again. Fletch noticed that Leary's shirt and jeans were so muddy and torn the signs identifying him as a convict were invisible. "Who's he? Is he goin' to be workin' here?"

"No," Fletch answered. "In fact, Emory, I want you to do this for me. Go get the truck and put the cattle grills on it." The grills were steel bars that would make a pen, nine feet high, all three sides, on the back of the pickup truck. "Throw a couple of small bales of hay on it. Then put that calf bull aboard, that little bastard who's discovered he can walk through barbed wire fences. Then put the truck up near the house, in the shade."

Jack muttered, "Wish you wouldn't be so free with the word *bastard.*"

"Sorry, Coitus Interruptus."

Emory started to move toward the house to get the truck. "You heard the news yet this mornin'?" He appeared to be asking his boots.

"No," Fletch answered. "Anything interesting?"

Emory turned around and walked backward. "Something about escaped convicts. Nine or ten of them. From Missouri, or some such place. They say they're here somewhere in the county."

"Oh, sure," Fletch said. "They always have to make a story, don't they? Just to frighten the horses. By

o◯ooo◯ooo◯o

the way, Emory, Carrie will be deliverin' the bull
for me, and I'll be takin' Jack here down to the
University of North Alabama. If anyone's lookin'
for us."

"Not to worry." Emory turned around to walk
frontward over the bridge. "I brought my gun."

Driving the truck, Emory passed Fletch and Jack
herding Leary toward the back of the house.

In the kitchen, Fletch said to Carrie, "The third
one is outside. His name is Leary. I told Jack to get
him stripped and hose him down."

Carrie looked through the kitchen window. "Big.
Ugly."

"Stupid."

In low voices, while cooking together, Fletch out-
lined his thoughts regarding the truck, the bull calf,
Leary, Carrie; the station wagon, Jack, Kriegel, himself. Carrie not only agreed, she relished the plan.
She refined a few of its elements.

They focused on what they did not yet know.

Outside the back door, Fletch waited for Jack to
turn off the hose before handing him a plate of ham
and eggs. Standing in the morning sunlight, Jack
proceeded to eat his breakfast.

When Fletch handed Leary his breakfast, Leary
sat cross-legged on the grassy slope, naked and
wet, to eat. Obviously he had lifted weights at
one time. Most of his bulk had slipped into his
gut, ass, thighs. His skin was pure white. He
seemed to wrap his whole body around his plate
of food.

He looked like a huge, hairless, white baby.

Fletch dropped a big garbage bag on the ground.

oᴑᴑᴑꝋᴑᴑᴑᴑꝋᴑᴑᴑo

He said to Jack, "Put everyone's clothes and boots in this."

"Then what do I do with it?"

"I haven't figured that out yet. The cops will be here later. To collect Moreno."

Jack looked up at him. "Just Moreno?"

"The rest of you will be gone by then. By the way, where are we really going?"

"Uh? South."

Fletch repeated, "Where are we really going?"

"Tolliver, Alabama. There's a camp there. In the woods. You know where Tolliver is?"

"Yes. Are you expected there?"

"Kriegel is."

"What kind of a camp? Boy Scout?"

"The Tribe." Jack watched Fletch's face.

"The Tribe? What's that when it's at home?"

"If you don't know," Jack said, "you'll find out. I want you to find out."

"A grand bunch of sterling chaps, I'm sure."

"Sure," Jack said. "Like a hunting camp, you know?"

"Paramilitary? Do they have a good marching band?"

"By the way, may I bring the guitar?"

"That will be nice. You can lead the singing around the campfire. I'll bring the marshmallows."

In the morning light, Jack was squinting at Fletch's face.

Fletch asked, "If you're Kriegel's lieutenant, what's Leary's function?"

"Bodyguard."

"Kriegel's bodyguard?"

o❍❍oo❍oo❍o

"Yeah."

Fletch nodded at the big baby sitting naked on the grass. He had dropped scrambled egg onto his stomach. With his hand he had slathered it up onto his chest. "I can see he would be good at that. Who wouldn't want to stay away from him? Did he kidnap someone because he was lonely?"

"I think you're about right," Jack said.

"Whom did he kidnap?"

"A teenaged girl. I think he thought they were eloping."

"She didn't think so?"

"No. And he carried her across a state line."

"The Mann Act. Did he rape her?"

"I think he thought he was making love. He kept her three weeks in a school bus. When he finally understood she didn't like him, he went to a pool hall and tried to sell her."

"His feelings were hurt."

"Again I think you're right."

Leary must have been hearing them talking about him. He never even looked up. He kept scoffing his food with his fingers.

Jack said, "You might say he just didn't know how to do things right."

Watching Leary eat, hearing about him, Fletch's stomach churned. "Not properly brought up, you might say."

Jack said, "You might say that."

"And Moreno?" Fletch asked. "What was his role in this scheme?"

"Money. He had a stash of it. In Florida."

"Drug money?"

o◯oo◯oo◯o

"Yeah."

"You all were going to rob him?"

"Rob him? He owed us." Jack grinned. "Then we were going to rob him. Once we knew how to get to his money."

"For a guitar picker, you sure know some different scales." Avoiding the puddles, Fletch walked toward the smokehouse.

"Hey," Jack said. "Don't I get any coffee?"

"You drink coffee?"

"Sure."

"You can go in the house. Ask Carrie to help you find some clothes for your traveling companions. White shirt, decent slacks for Kriegel, maybe a necktie. Overalls for Leary. I don't want Leary wearing a shirt."

Glancing at Leary's blubber, Jack muttered, "I do."

"We are sorry, but due to seismic disturbances, your telephone call to this exchange in California cannot be completed at this time. Please try your call at a later time."

"Wow." Fletch was in the smokehouse, with the door closed, using his cellular phone. " 'Seismic disturbances'! They're so used to California rockin' and rollin' they're ready with a recorded message! A recorded message about seismic disturbances! So cool! *We are sorry*"— Fletch imitated the computer voice— "*as California has just crumbled into the ocean and whoever you are calling doubtlessly has just been swallowed by earth, fire, or water, we are unable to complete your call. Have a nice day!* Should

o⊂◯oo◯oo◯o

have called Andy Cyst in the first place. Last night."

While punching in Alston Chambers's home telephone number, Fletch had felt a twinge of guilt. He was sure he would be waking Alston and his whole family. He assuaged his guilt by telling himself that matters had gotten to such a point at the farm, his inferences had been so unsettling, especially regarding a son, *Crystal's son*—to say nothing of his having a murderer, a rapist-kidnapper, an attempted murderer, and a corpse underfoot; that he was apparently aiding these fugitives from justice; that he was going somewhere, being taken somewhere of which he was distinctly unsure; that now Carrie was involved, however gladly, whimsically in his reaching out to his son, *Crystal's son,* his trying to discover the truth about him, perhaps irrationally risking too much for someone essentially a stranger with a poor résumé, desperately he needed factual information. From the telephone company's recorded message, Fletch now assumed Alston and his family were up. Or down. Or in or out.

Now punching in Andy Cyst's home telephone number in Virginia, California passed before Fletch's eyes: some of his life, experiences there; some of his friends, people he loved, others.

What was happening to them?

Andy answered on the first ring. "Hello?"

"Andy, what's happening in California?"

"Aftershocks?" Andy answered. "Foreshocks? Another of the big ones? Geologists, as you know, Mister Fletcher, are slow to commit to their jargon."

"Any real damage reported?"

o◯oo◯oo◯o

"Many communication lines aren't working. So we don't know. This series started just an hour ago. Where are you?"

"At the farm. I'm not really calling about California."

"Good." Andy's voice was always eager. Not this morning. "Ask me something I know."

"Andy, you don't sound like your old self."

"I'm fine."

"A little irascible?"

"Just fine."

Having been a print journalist, and someone who had written a book, Fletch persisted in believing there was not much future in electronics, generally. Therefore, in an effort to dispose of some money he never was sure he deserved, many years previously he had invested in a start-up business called Global Cable News.

On his last visit to their offices three years previous, he discovered that since Global Cable's move from Washington, D.C., to deep in the Virginia countryside, their headquarters had grown to airport-hangar size. Besides the studios, there were rows and rows of young people frowning at computer workstations. There were whole sections of medical doctors working as journalists, lawyers working as journalists, people with doctors of philosophy in the various disciplines working as journalists, athletes working as journalists. They did not seem to talk to each other. NO SMOKING signs were everywhere. There were neither wads of chewing tobacco nor chewing gum on the floors. The windows were clean. The facility had a health spa, including trainers,

oC○ooC○ooC○o

handball courts, and an Olympic-sized swimming pool, and a day-care center. Just the parking lot was acres big.

As a journalist, Fletch had worked (as seldom as possible) in a city room in a building he thought big in the busiest section of the city, surrounded by bars and theaters and bars and police stations and bars and slums. Few journalists had academic degrees. They had strong legs, loud voices, no regard for theories, predictions, speculation, trends, or statistics. They believed only in discovering and printing the facts of present history. They lived in the city, rode the buses, the subways, hung around the bars, police stations, hospitals, ballparks, political enclaves. They had charm and temper and the gift of gab that would draw admissions from a judge. They loved and hated each other with passion.

News, in those days, was ninety-five percent fact, three percent fancy, and two percent speculation.

As extrapolation had not yet entered the business, news, in those days, was far less confusing.

When Fletch would call Global Cable News with a bit of information, *news,* suggestion, comment, a question, he was answered with *Yes, Mister Fletcher. Yes, Mister Fletcher. Yes, Mister Fletcher,* instant response, thorough follow-through. It made him as uncomfortable as their headquarters. He did not like being listened to as a journalist because he was a major investor.

So he asked that when he called, only one person answer and say, *Yes, Mister Fletcher.*

That person was Andy Cyst.

"Yes, Mister Fletcher?"

"Andy, I need some information. First, I need to find a woman named Crystal Faoni." He spelled the name out. "She used to be a working journalist. I believe she never married. I believe she has one son, named John, which she has raised herself. I'm told she now owns five radio stations in Indiana. Possibly with a residence in Bloomington. Presently, she may be at a health spa, I'm told *incommunicado,* somewhere."

"F-A-O-N-I?"

"Yes."

"An unusual name."

"I'm afraid so."

"An old flame, eh?" Andy asked.

"An old spark, more like."

"Why do you need me? You have enough information here—"

"Because I am limited in what I can do at this moment." He hoped Andy was saying to himself, *The old boy's gettin' lazy.* "Also, I think I would like to see, or at least talk to, Faoni within the next few days. Where exactly is she? What's her schedule? How serious is this *incommunicado* situation? When you find her."

"Okay."

"Next, some convicts escaped from the federal penitentiary in Tomaston, Kentucky, yesterday."

"Yes. Two."

"Two?"

"I'm trying to recall what I saw regarding this story on Global Cable News. We've carried the full story, needless to say."

o☾oo◯oo☾o

"Andy, you know I don't get cable here on the farm."

"I know."

"Cable was originally intended for rural areas. Then your business chiefs discovered dwellings in the cities and towns are closer together, and therefore much more profitable to wire. So we still don't get cable out here."

"You've mentioned this to me before."

"About a thousand times."

"Thirteen hundred and five times. You're the one who makes the profits, Mister Fletcher."

"Go ahead. Rub it in. I just want you all to know why I am not a devoted viewer. Why I do not memorize your every shifting probability. Furthermore, I understand there are four escapees." To himself, Fletch said, *Now there are three.* "I need to know everything about every one of them."

"Are you working on something, Mister Fletcher? I mean, for GCN?"

"Just maybe."

"You want a crew?"

"No. Not yet, anyway. Was anyone hurt during the escape?"

"Ummm. I think not. You want me to boot up my personal computer to read the office files?"

"No. I haven't the time right now. I have another call to make."

"Sorry, I guess I didn't pay that much attention to this story. Last night we, uh—"

Fletch waited. "Are you going to tell me?"

"Went to a concert, in old D.C."

"So you had a late night."

"You know what was weird?"

o〇ooo〇ooo〇o

"Tell me." In the smokehouse, Fletch glanced at his watch.

"The first half of the concert was big band, you know, like in the 1940s? The second half a rock light show. Like in the sixties, I guess."

"Eclectic," Fletch said.

"It's left me confused. Headachy."

One of many things Fletch admired about Andy was his respect for straight lines. "Go with the flow, baby."

"Anything else? I'm leaving for the office now."

"What's The Tribe?"

"Whose?"

"I guess that's the right question."

"Mister Fletcher, I told you I heard more noise last night than is good for one."

"I know, Andy. You lead the quiet life, there in the Virginia countryside."

"Is this a real question? Am I supposed to find out something about some tribe?"

"I don't know yet. But the question doesn't mean anything to you?"

"Can noise make you feel sort of sick? We had beef Thai pecan last night, wild rice. That couldn't have done it, could it?"

"As long as the pecans weren't wild."

"Are there wild pecans?"

"Oh, Andy, you should know some of the nuts I've known! I'll say they can be wild! I'll call you later at the office. Don't try to call me."

"Hi, Aetna. Will you patch me through to the sheriff, please?"

oᴑooᴑooᴑo

"Hydy, Mister Fletcher. How's everything at the farm this fine morning? You all survive the big storm last night?"

"Just fine, Aetna. We're as slick as a boxer after the tenth round."

Fletch wondered if the dispatcher for the county sheriff's office recognized the voice of everyone in the county. Once, only by recognizing a woman's voice had she sent the Rescue Squad to the right farm. She was credited with saving the woman's life. She also had a great ear for music. She led the county's most accomplished Baptist choir.

"The sheriff's actin' right tired this morning, Mister Fletcher."

"I expect so."

"Say, Mister Fletcher, while I have you on the phone, will you tell Carrie that Angie Kelly has that recipe for firecracker cake Carrie wanted?"

"Angie Kelly. Firecracker cake."

"Who's talking about firecracker cake on this line?"

Fletch recognized Sheriff Rogers's gravelly voice. It was more gravelly than usual this morning.

Aetna said, "Mister Fletcher's on the line, Sheriff."

The sheriff said, "I sincerely doubt Mister Fletcher is interested in the recipe for firecracker cake."

Fletch said, "I don't even know what firecracker cake is. Listen, Sheriff, I have two of them."

"Cakes?"

"Convicts. Escaped convicts."

"Where?"

"One of them is dead. We found him in the gully

behind my barns. Looks like the snakes got him, and then maybe he drowned."

"Describe him."

"Hispanic."

"I'm prepared to call that a good arrest, aren't you?"

"Absolutely."

"Describe the other convict to me."

"Heavyset. Caucasian. None too bright."

"Okay. Restrain him however you can. We'll come pick him up."

"Please, no."

"No?"

"Carrie is going to drive him out to the intersection of Worthy Road and The Old County Pike. He'll be penned up in the back of the pickup truck. She'll pretend she's run out of gas. As soon as she stops at the intersection there, you guys swarm him."

"Why you want to do it that way? Why don't we just come shoot the bastard your place?"

"I don't particularly want that to happen."

"Oh, I see. Sorry, Fletch. Your wife. Princess . . . You don't want the unpleasantness of a police action your place. Might attract the tourists, uh? Cause the press to reprise the assassination. Is that it?"

"Something like that." One way and another, Fletch had learned the importance of creating a diversion.

"We do it my way, he'll be docile. We're telling him Carrie is helping him escape. He's a real big guy. He'll be half asleep. This way, all you need do is step out of the woods, swarm him, and chain him."

"Sure." The sheriff was slurring his words, just

oᏦoooᏦoooᏦo

slightly. "We'll blow him away wherever you say."

"Carrie doesn't particularly need to see anyone blown away, either, here, there, or anywhere."

"Okay. I understand. We've got to protect the ladies." The sheriff burped. "And their gardens. We'll tiptoe out of the woods and take him off Carrie's truck as gently as a potted petunia. Say again where she will be?"

"At the intersection of Worthy Road and Old County Pike. She'll be there at nine o'clock sharp."

"Okay. Nine o'clock sharp."

This rank, nonsensical interference in normal police procedure was proving easier than Fletch had thought.

"Worthy Road and Old County Pike, nine o'clock," Fletch repeated.

"I've got it. We'll be there. In tennis shoes."

"By the way, Sheriff, will you do me a favor?"

"Anything."

"This morning I'm driving my son and his professor down to the University of North Alabama. In the station wagon. They absolutely have to be there by eleven o'clock. Will you tell your guys and the state troopers please to let us through any roadblocks without delay?"

"Sure. I even recall your vanity license plate. I'll put that on the radio right away. After what you've done: capturin' those two guys. We've been up all night."

"Sorry. You must be tired."

"Rain that hard, ordinarily I would have called the hunt off. Sent everybody home. I mean, if we were just huntin' ornery critters."

o◖◦◦◖◦◦◖o

"There will be three of us in the car. And Carrie will meet you at Worthy Road and Old Pike intersection at nine o'clock exactly."

"This is great!" the sheriff said. "Only one left!"

The line went dead before Fletch could check the sheriff's arithmetic.

oᗧᗧoᗧᗧOᗧoᗧo

chapter 8

"Your name is Carrie?"

Not having heard him enter the kitchen, she was leaning over, putting a frying pan in the dishwasher. When she stood up, her tanned face was slightly reddened, not, Jack suspected, from exertion.

"Broom Hilda," Carrie said. "I'm a witch."

Jack dropped two paper plates and a plastic knife and fork into the wastebasket by the back door of the kitchen. "That was Kriegel who said that."

"There's a difference?" Carrie said.

"Yes," Jack said. "There's a difference."

"He's soft. Ugly. Sayin' things that aren't polite don't make any more sense than fleas bitin' a shag rug."

"And I am . . . " Jack stood, the light in the opened back door behind him, in the coolness of the kitchen. " . . . What?"

Arms akimbo, Carrie said, "What are you? Only God and you know that, and I suspect you're confused."

"Confused?" Jack seemed to consider the question. "Maybe. I don't think so. Maybe I'm not what you think I am."

"Not Fletch's son?"

"I'm Fletch's son. You said yourself we look alike. Have the same bodies. Builds. Whatever you said."

"You surely do favor him. You're standin' there fifteen feet away from me, head down a little bit, starin' at me half-solemn, half-humorous, hands at your sides, all-neat and all-gangly at the same time just the way Fletch did before we ever touched each other. And a million times since." Carrie asked, "Are you comin' on to me, boy?"

"No, ma'am. I'm surely not."

"You speak Southern pretty good, too, when you want to. I had to teach Fletch, and he never will get it right."

"You must love him," Jack said.

"Because I teach him Southern ways?"

"Because you're putting up with our being here." He grinned. "Because you haven't shot any of us yet. Course, I haven't seen Kriegel lately."

"He's sleepin' the sleep of the unjust. Does it surprise you, our puttin' up with you all the way we're doin'?"

"No. It's what I expected. From him. He has a reputation for being curious."

o◯∞◯∞◯o

"Peculiar, you mean. We're not at all afraid of you bunch, you know."

"Clearly not."

"Should we be?"

"Not of me." Jack glanced through the windows. Outside, on the grassy slope, Leary slept. "As for the others, for a reason I've just recently figured out, they seem peculiarly weary this morning. Weak. Or dead. They spent the night in a gully fighting off snakes, rushing water, and God knows what else."

Across the kitchen, Jack and Carrie gave each other a smile as brief as a glance.

"What does puzzle me," Jack said, "is your manners. The manners of both of you."

"Come again?"

"Neither one of you has said to me, simply, 'Hello. How are you?'"

Carrie asked, "Did you or did you not arrive here out of a storm in the middle of the night, carryin' three desperadoes with you?"

"Still . . ."

"I didn't hear that you exactly knocked politely on the front door and came in all full of smiles sayin', 'Hello, I'm your son, Jack. How are you?' Did you?"

"Not exactly."

"Besides," Carrie answered in a milder tone, "generally, Fletch doesn't hold much stock in simple questions. He says, when you ask a question all you get is an answer to the question, not the truth. He says, to get the truth it's best to wait and watch and listen."

"Oh, yes," Jack said. "I have heard that about him."

o◯oo◯oo◯o

"From your mother?"

"Yes. And others."

"Did your mother love Fletch?"

"Yes."

"Does she still?"

"Yes. And me."

"What does she say about your bein' put in prison? I'll bet she's proud."

Jack turned his face away from her. "I'll bet she is."

"Well." Carrie sighed. "One thing is sure about Mister Fletch. We're goin' to understand all this before we're done, or die tryin'. And that includes you."

Jack asked, "Why don't you ask me how I feel?"

"About what?"

Jack lifted his arms from his sides. "About everything."

"Oh, yes," Carrie said. "Fletch calls you *the tactile generation.* For short, he calls you the *scabpickers.* What you know, what you do isn't important, only what you *feel.* Well, let me tell you somethin', boy: What you feel is important, all right, but there isn't enough time on earth to know or care about all that you feel."

Jack stared at her. "Suppress feelings?"

"No, of course not," Carrie said. "Take a potshot at a woman cop because you feel like it. Maybe you'll get to go on a teevee talk show so you can talk about your feelin's. For fifteen minutes some people will say, 'Poor you,' and you'll still end up in the jailhouse." More gently, she said, "So how do you feel?"

"Weird," Jack said. "I just met my father for the first time. I just met you. I see this place where you

oꙨooꙨooꙨo

live." He waved one arm. "You've got horses that sneak up behind you in the dark of the night and try to nibble the hair off your head! You've got goddamned oil paintings on the walls of your kitchen!"

"$E=MC^2$!" Carrie expostulated. "Don't you swear in front of me!"

"Swear! He had me put my 'traveling companions,' as he calls them, in a gully in a raging storm. He killed one and beat up the other two as surely as if he took a bat to them, and he never lifted a finger. My father!"

"Scared?" Carrie asked.

Jack took a deep breath. "I knew what I was thinking when I headed this way."

"Well," Carrie said, "I surely don't, but I've had enough of you and your feelings for now. We've got things to do."

"Yeah," Jack said. "Clothes."

"There's a pair of huge overalls somewhere there in the back closet, left here by a hired hand the whole county couldn't afford to feed. Sent him to Kansas. Maybe if we split them down the sides we can make them fit that nasty-lookin' thing asleep on the grass outside feedin' the ticks and fleas."

Jack looked through the window. "He's not feedin' anything."

"Oh, yes he is."

"He said something about a suit for Kriegel. Shirt. Necktie."

"I'll take care of that," Carrie said. "I'll go wake Kriegel up. I look forward to givin' him his breakfast. How'd you like that country ham you had for breakfast?"

o☰oooO☰oo

"Salty."

"You want some more?"

"Not just now, thanks."

"Okay," Carrie said. "You can tell me how you feel about that ham later."

oOooOooOo

chapter 9

"By golly, Ms. Carrie," Fletch said, bounding into the dining room where Professor The Reverend Doctor Kris Kriegel breakfasted in state. "We've never had houseguests so plumb worn out in the mornings before, I do declare!"

In a white shirt, purple necktie, dark trousers, Kriegel sat at the head of the long, highly polished dining table. On his place mat was a full china breakfast setting, silver cutlery. At almost full attention, Jack stood beside, a little behind him.

"More ham?" Carrie asked the rotund little man.

"Please." His pale blue eyes gazed over the saddle-shaped birthmark over the bridge of his nose. "It is most delicious."

Carrie heaped more of the ham on his plate.

"All three hundred and fifty pounds of white and naked flab you all call Leary is dead to the world out on the back lawn," Fletch said. "I swear, if we drag him down to the roadside, the slaughter truck will pick him up for the glue factory without even stopping to ask which nature of beast he is."

"Speaking of dead—" Kriegel began.

"By the way," Fletch said to Carrie, ignoring him, "I forgot to tell you Aetna says Angie Kelly has that recipe for firecracker cake you want."

Carrie's lips twitched. She knew Fletch had made his arrangements with the sheriff's department.

Jack glanced from one to the other. Clearly he knew some message had just passed subtly between them.

He did not ask.

Kriegel cleared his throat. "Speaking of dead," he began again.

"Yes?" Fletch asked.

Frowning as if at an underling, Kriegel said to Fletch, "You may have deprived me—you have deprived us—of a very important source of revenue."

"Us?" Fletch asked. "You mean me, too?"

"The late Juan Moreno, or so he was known in this country—"

"Yes," Fletch said. "John Brown. Go on."

"—is lamented principally for the cash he was going to provide us."

"Is a-moldering in the ditch," said Fletch.

"He was indebted to us, you see, for our allowing him to escape with us the confines of the federal penitentiary. He was to pay us from his considerable funds deposited in various Florida banks. Now that he is dead, these funds may be harder for us, even impossible, to tap."

"The snakes got him," Fletch said simply.

Kriegel placed his cloth napkin on the table. "That," he announced, "was the worst night of my entire life. Whose idea was it to conceal me in that raging river filled with barbed wire, old washtubs, and enormous snakes floating down on us in squadrons so thick they were actually entangled with each other?" His voice broke.

"Mine," Fletch said.

Kriegel was trying to glare with his watery blue eyes. "I barely survived the experience. Only my call saved me."

"Your cowl?"

"My calling!"

"Exactly," Fletch said. "The cops didn't cotch you. In fact, they did look everywhere else."

"But only, I understand, Mister Fletcher, because you provided them with the use of your four-wheel-drive Jeep to search for us!"

"Certainly," said Fletch. "I always cooperate with the coppers. They're my friends. They do their best to keep murdering loonies like you locked up."

"Mister Fletcher." Despite his agitation, Fletch could see Kriegel was having difficulty keeping his eyes open. "I happen to be a political figure of international significance, and require that I be treated as such, with all due respect."

Carrie cut her eyes at Fletch. Personages of genuine international political significance had sat at

oOooOoooOo

that table many times. None had required particular respect, even during one or two memorable bread fights.

"I am of such significance that your American authorities, in their wisdom, decided it their best course of action to imprison me on perfectly irrelevant criminal charges."

"I know," Fletch said in a sympathetic tone. "Both that whore who strangled herself on your bed and that chambermaid who walked in on you and saw what had happened were government agents. They're everywhere, they are. You don't need to tell me."

"I said, 'irrelevant.' "

"I understand," Fletch said. "The strangled whore was irrelevant to your call."

"Exactly."

Carrie said, "The whore had a calling, too."

"What difference did the life of a whore make considering the scope of my mission?"

"What's your mission?" Fletch asked.

"At the moment, my mission is to get to my people who await me." Tiredly, Kriegel stood up.

"More ham?" Carrie asked.

"Thank you, no."

"We've got that all worked out." Fletch pulled a torn road map from his back pocket. He spread it on the dining table. "We have to split you up. There are roadblocks everywhere looking for you three. Four. Pretending to drive my son, Jack, to the University of North Alabama, you, Jack, and I, in the station wagon, will take this road into Alabama, you see? and then turn east to Tolliver."

oOooOooOo

Carrie was watching Fletch's fingers on the map.

Bleary from exhaustion, Kriegel was not focusing successfully. "What of my bodyguard?" Kriegel asked. "What of Mister Leary?"

"Ah," Fletch said. "That's the beauty of the plan. Mister Leary will be going in the pickup truck with Ms. Carrie. She is going to pretend to be delivering a little cow. Dressed as a farm worker, he will ride on the back of the truck with the little cow. She will take these back roads in an arc, you see? And meet us in Tolliver. That way we won't all be traveling together."

Kriegel looked at Carrie's 123 pounds on a five-foot-five frame. "I see. But I do not wish to be separated from my bodyguard."

"Come, come," Fletch said. "Jack and I will be with you. What have you to fear? You know Jack is a karate expert. And I? Don't even ask. Never have I met man or beast to make me tremble in nose or lip."

"Will you be armed?" Kriegel asked in a high voice.

"Indeed not," Fletch answered. "The worst thing we could do would be to carry arms." He had already put the .32 he had given Jack (which Fletch found under the afghan on the study's divan), properly loaded, and the cellular phone under the driver's seat of the station wagon. He had put the loaded .38 under the driver's seat of the truck. "We'll be going through roadblocks. Cops find weapons on us they'll nab us for sure. They'd have you back in Tomaston before lunch. Pity if you escaped prison just for a zoological experience in a ditch."

oꙨ∞Ꙩ∞Ꙩo

Kriegel wished to be armed against the authorities.

Fletch wished himself and Carrie to be armed against Kriegel and Leary.

If biff came to bang, Fletch would be interested to see what John Fletcher Faoni would do.

Kriegel said, "I want my own bodyguard with me."

"What?" Fletch asked. "Are you saying you don't trust Jack?"

"It's not that," Kriegel said. "I need my bodyguard."

"You're not grasping the beauty of this plan," Fletch said.

"What's the beauty?" Kriegel rubbed his face.

"Leary," Fletch said. "Leary is the beauty."

"Leary is a beauty?" asked Kriegel.

"Oh, yes." Fletch said: "Bait."

"Bait!" Kriegel said.

"If the cops should happen to catch him over here"—Fletch fingered Carrie's route—"we'll have a clearer road over here." He fingered his own route.

"Oh, yes." Kriegel looked around anxiously. He whispered, "Can he hear us?"

"He's asleep." Fletch had been certain Kriegel would no more mind throwing Leary to the cops to save his own freedom than Fletch had minded throwing all three of them to the snakes.

"Yes, I see," Kriegel said.

"Wasn't it Julius Caesar," Fletch asked, "who said something about divide and skinny through?"

"He said, 'All roads lead to Rome.' "

"That, too," Fletch agreed. "Quite a phrasemaker,

that Caesar feller. I knew you know your military history."

"Oh, yes," said Kriegel.

Fletch folded up the torn map. "Right! We'd better get going. Your followers await you."

"Get aboard," Fletch said to Leary.

"How?"

In the driveway, Leary looked at the tall steel pen rising up from the back of the pickup truck. He was wearing Fletch's rubber boots and the overalls split down to his thighs. The overalls were held up by straps over his shirtless shoulders.

"Oh, yeah," Fletch said as if he had not considered the matter before. "You're too big to climb over the grill, aren't you?"

"What's that?" Leary pointed at the 450-pound bull calf already in the pen on the back of the truck.

"A little cow," Fletch said.

"Why can't I ride up front with the lady?" Leary asked.

"Because you have to hold on to the little cow," Fletch said. "You don't want it to get hurt, do you?"

"No."

"I didn't think so. See, there's hay there. You feed the little cow the hay as you go along."

"Does the little cow need the hay as we go along?"

"You don't think Ms. Carrie can drive the truck and feed the little cow hay at the same time, do you?"

"No."

"This is a real job of work you're doin'."

"Oh."

oOooOooOo

"The cops will never recognize you this way."

"No."

"This is a great disguise, you see."

"Yeah."

"And Ms. Carrie can't reach back and hold on to the little cow, can she?"

"No," Leary agreed. "I can see that."

"So you have to ride in back with the little cow."

"I don't know," Leary said. In the morning sunlight, sweat already was pouring down his fat, white skin.

Jack was standing at the back of the truck watching.

Kriegel had come out of the house and immediately slumped into the backseat of the station wagon. He sat with his head leaning on the palm of one hand.

Fletch stepped close to Leary and said, softly, "You're not afraid, are you? Of that little cow?"

"Of course not!" Leary shouted.

With the driver's door open, Carrie said, "We've got to get goin'."

"Here, Jack." Fletch grabbed the steel bars on one side of the rear grill. "Help me lift this up."

They lifted that section of the grill just high enough for Leary to crawl under it onto the truck.

"Come on!" Fletch said sharply. "We can't hold this thing all day! Get aboard, or I'll put you down in the henhouse with the rest of the chickens!"

The bull calf, seeing the opening, tried to get under the grill to get off the truck.

Leary, crawling under the grill onto the truck, butted heads with the bull calf.

oOooOooOo

Neither expressed surprise or pain.

Fletch and Jack dropped the stanchions of the grill section into their deep holes.

Carrie gave Fletch a wide, delighted grin before stepping into the truck and starting the engine.

Fletch shouted at Leary, "Now, hold on to that little cow!"

Standing, with his feet spread, Leary grabbed the bull calf's tail.

As Carrie started the truck down the driveway, Leary's boots slipped in wet manure already on the floor of the pickup truck's bed. He landed on his ass. On the manure.

Both his hands still held on to the bull calf's tail.

"Hold on to it!" Fletch ordered.

"It's shittin' on me!" Leary yelled halfway down the driveway.

It certainly was.

Jack turned his back to the station wagon. Keeping his back, his shoulders steady, arms at his sides, he was laughing hard but silently.

Fletch watched Carrie drive the truck along the road out of sight. Leary was trying to stand up, regain his footing on the manure on the floor of the truck's bed. He was doing a good job of holding on to the bull calf's tail.

For his efforts he was getting liberally sprayed with wet dung.

Then Fletch watched Jack choking with laughter.

"Oh, hello." Fletch slapped Jack on the back. "How are you feeling?"

chapter 10

"Thirsty," Jack said.

"Really?" Fletch said. "How could that be? Why, you're not even as warm as last night's pizza yet."

He was driving with the windows open. The station wagon's air conditioner was not on.

From the car's passenger seat, Jack watched Fletch's face. "I wonder how Carrie and Leary are doing."

The dashboard clock said nine-fifteen. If all had gone well, Leary was in chains in the back of a police car on his way back to prison. Carrie was on her way back to the farm. The bull calf was on his way back to pasture, of course having no idea why he had been loaded on a truck and taken for a ride to nowhere that morning.

If all had gone well.

Jack looked into the backseat where Professor The Reverend Doctor Kris Kriegel slept soundly. His pudgy hands were folded in his lap. He snored.

Jack said, "Leary certainly was a sight, being dragged down the road in a pen on the back of Carrie's truck, being shit on and kicked by that young bull all the way."

"Wasn't he though?" Fletch agreed. "I wonder if he felt anything at all like that young woman he kidnapped?"

Jack smiled. "Shall I sing a few bars of 'Let the Punishment Fit the Crime'?"

"Can you?"

"No."

"That's good."

Jack said, "I'm amazed at the way you have kept us all weak, incapacitated."

"All?"

"Not Moreno, of course. Him you got killed."

"Are you incapacitated?"

"No," Jack said. "Why aren't I? Why didn't you put me in the gully, too? You could have talked me into it." Fletch did not answer. "I know. Because you're curious. 'Mildly curious' about me. You want to see what I will do. Do you think you can handle me? Or is it that you trust me?"

"Neither."

"So you're just taking a chance with me."

"A very big chance."

Rounding a curve in the road, they came across a dozen vehicles lined up, stopped. They were waiting to go through a roadblock.

oOooOooOo

Fletch slowed the station wagon but proceeded up the left lane.

"What are you doing?" Jack asked in alarm.

"Not waiting for the roadblock. I hope my neighbors don't think me arrogant. Can't quite explain to them I have the fugitives the cops are looking for, can I?"

"Are you turning us in?"

His arm out the window, Fletch waved at Deputy Michael Jackson.

Michael waved back and shouted, "Hey, wait!"

Fletch stopped. He cursed himself for not putting luggage in the car. Then he remembered he had left the garbage bag full of prison clothes and boots outside his back door, and he cursed himself again.

Michael put his hands on the windowsill of the door beside Jack. "Hey, Jack. Are you going to be home next weekend?"

"Maybe," Jack said. "I'm not sure."

"I'm off duty next Saturday, and there's a party down at the river. Want to come?"

"Sounds good."

"Girls," Michael said.

"Sounds better."

"You might bring your guitar."

"Okay."

"I'll call your dad." Michael looked into the backseat. "Who's that?"

In the backseat, blinking slowly, Kriegel was waking up. The guitar was propped up on the seat beside him. Their shapes were similar. The guitar had the more attractive neck.

Fletch said, "That's Jack's teacher. Professor Josiah Black. We just picked him up this morning."

"Good morning, sir," Michael said.

Kriegel said, "I'm very thirsty."

"How do you feel this morning, Michael?" Fletch asked.

The deputy stuck his fingers between his collar and his neck. "Still wet. Thanks for the coffee last night, Mister Fletcher. Sammy and Bobby are using your Jeep this morning. They're still up by your place."

"No harm done?"

"Began slidin' downhill once and almost tipped over once, but other than that, we're fine. That Jeep is fun!" Michael slapped the side of the station wagon, as he would the flank of a horse. "Well, don't mean to hold you up. See you next Saturday, Jack."

As Fletch worked his way through the roadblock, Jack waved his arm out the window at the deputy.

Then he returned to watching Fletch's face. "Glad he didn't hold us up any."

"Nice of him," Fletch agreed.

Kriegel cleared his throat. "I am very thirsty, I said."

Fletch said, "Oh."

Kriegel asked, "Who is this Professor Josiah Black?"

Neither Fletch nor Jack answered.

Kriegel insisted. "What did you mean by 'Josiah Black'?"

Fletch did not answer.

"It comes from an old American song, sir," Jack answered.

o☾∘∘☾∘∘☾o

"What's the name of the song?"

Jack said, " 'Ol' Black Joe.' "

" 'Ol' Black Joe'?" Kriegel spluttered. "You called me an old, black Joe? Is that supposed to be funny?"

"I had to tell him something, didn't I?" Fletch asked. "Couldn't say you are Santa Claus now, could I?"

"Mister Fletcher," Kriegel intoned, "whether you like it or not, you are a member of our tribe."

"What tribe is that?" Fletch asked.

Kriegel took a moment to collect his thoughts. "How do you feel?"

"Fine."

"I mean, don't you realize you are the most despised person on earth?"

"Who, me?"

"You are the intelligent, educated to some degree, I gather, well-off, middle-aged, heterosexual white male. On this earth, you are distinctly the minority. Yet you and your kind have made the world, as we know it, what it is. For centuries, you have created the religious and political institutions, the businesses, the wars, laws that protect and suit you to the exclusion of others, while exploiting all people of color, Indians, Negroids, Orientals, even those less fortunate than yourself of the same tribe, the laborers, as well as all women and children."

"Wow." Fletch well knew these sentiments. He had been confronted with such often enough. "And all this time I thought I was just gettin' along best I could."

"Do you consider yourself 'responsible'?"

o〇oo〇oo〇o

"Oh, yes."

"According to current cant, you are responsible for everything wrong with the world. Being 'responsible,' so it is said, is just your rationalization for controlling everyone else in the world, so you can have everything your way. The whole world is rebelling against you, Mister Fletcher. The women, the children, the Indians, the Negroids, the Orientals, and even some of your own kind we shall call here *the liberals.*" His voice dripped irony. "How do you feel, being so despised?"

Driving the station wagon, Fletch said nothing.

"Have you ever stopped to ask yourself," Kriegel continued rhetorically, "why the Anglo-Saxon has had more than his share of the world's good fortune?"

Fletch yawned. "Why?"

"Because we, not the Jews, not the Moslems, not the people of color, are the true descendants of Abraham, Isaac, and Jacob."

" '$E=MC^2$,' " Fletch quoted.

"What?"

"Cool, clear water," Fletch sang.

Kriegel ran his tongue around inside his mouth. "How can I be so thirsty when I swallowed half a raging river last night?"

"You should have swallowed the other half, too."

"You had better consider this seriously, Mister Fletcher."

"What, your being thirsty? Chew buttons."

They crossed the border into Alabama. The land had flattened. There were wide cotton fields on both sides of the road.

o◖◦o◦◖◗◦◦o◗o

Dry-mouthed, Kriegel persisted lecturing in the backseat. "As the world's populations increase, as the world's resources decline, as the global economy thins, we, the true minority, are an endangered species. Within a few hundred years, if it takes that long, people like you will not exist. There will be chaos."

"That's quite a leap, isn't it?"

"The truth is, it is the white male, the Aryan, the Anglo-Saxon, who has brought the only real order to this earth that this earth has ever known."

"Oh, come now. What about Shaka Zulu?"

"Hear my word. This century some white people have tried to preach the equality of men and women, equality of the races, even the equality of children with adults. We must all live together in perfect harmony. Isn't that the way some popular song goes? Have you visited universities or prisons lately, Mister Fletcher?"

"In fact, I have," Fletch said. "Both."

"And have you seen that in the great bastions of higher learning—once the exclusive enclaves of white males—women, Negroids, Orientals, instead of integrating, have resegregated themselves into Women's Studies, Afro-American Studies, Asian Studies? They have established separate colleges within the existing university structures. There is no place from the Balkans to the city of Los Angeles where tribal wars are not raging. Am I right? Humans basically are tribal, Mister Fletcher, something your government does not understand. There is the individual. There is the family. There is the tribe. In this country, after these two hun-

oⵔ○oooⵔooⵔo

dred years of democracy, the melting pot, you see the family breaking down, as a result of these impossible ideas. Is it a good thing? The tribes aren't breaking down. They never will, anywhere in the world. Tribes support family. The family supports the individual. You had better realize to which tribe you belong, Mister Fletcher.

"God, am I thirsty."

"Are you, indeed?" Fletch asked.

"Terribly, terribly thirsty. Can't we stop for something to drink?"

"I don't think that would be wise. You didn't look half as nice in jailhouse denim, Doctor."

"I'm thirsty, too," Jack assured Kriegel. "I think it has something to do with the ham we had for breakfast."

Fletch aimed a wide grin at him.

Jack asked Fletch, "You didn't have any ham for breakfast, did you?"

"Just eggs and juice."

"What else are you doing to incapacitate us?"

Fletch threw him another wide grin.

"I've got to have something to drink," Kriegel said. "Soon."

"If, as you say," Fletch asked, "this tribal business is so natural, and happening anyway, why does it need encouragement?"

"We must protect ourselves, Mister Fletcher, to survive. We are the minority," Kriegel said. "Doesn't that frighten you?"

"Not really," Fletch said. "But then again, everyone likes me."

"It is natural to want one's own kind to survive."

o○○○○○○○○○

"I have a different view," Fletch said.

Through his dry throat, Kriegel said, patiently, "What would that be?"

"That tribalism is being used, around the world, by a lot of would-be tinpot demagogues and dictators, warlords, simply to grab power and all the good things for themselves. That is what really goes on in the world, among whites, blacks, Asians, women, children, always has and always will: power-mongering based on individual greed."

Kriegel said, "I'm too thirsty to talk more."

Fletch asked, "You don't want me to respond?"

"I can't think of any response you would have worth listening to." Kriegel sighed. "What experience have you of these matters?"

"Some." Fletch smiled. "For example, have you noticed that statistically the more separatism the worse the social, economic, health statistics regarding each underclass—women, children, gays, Afro-Americans, Jews, Native Americans, Asians—become in relation to the whole? Fractionalism, whatever, is like some kind of a weird, self-absorbing prism. It's like a family in which the members, instead of loving and supporting each other, are negative toward each other, are suspicious of each other, hateful, destructive. The individual suffers. The whole suffers. Haven't you noticed that?"

"As I said . . . "

Through the rearview mirror, Fletch watched Kriegel's eyes close again. Shortly, he was snoring.

"Ummm." Fletch smiled at Jack. "Not the first time I've noticed that those who lecture, frequently don't listen."

oC)ooC)ooC)o

What was weird to Fletch was that within that month, an Afro-American leader had sat with Fletch on the terrace behind the farmhouse and said much the same thing Kriegel had just said—only he said people of "Fletch's kind" would be extinct within 150 years.

Fletch was aware Jack was watching him.

Never had Fletch felt so studied.

Fletch said, "I've never been an easy convert."

Quietly, Jack asked, "Is it possible you're not listening?"

"I think I am. I think I have been. Listening and thinking. The Separate-but-Equal Doctrine was established in the 1896 United States Supreme Court decision *Plessy vs. Ferguson*. Thus were established the so-called Jim Crow Laws. At the time, I guess some thought it a big liberal leap forward. In the 1960s it was thought there could not be equality without integration. Then what? What has happened? Racism has taken off its coat," Fletch said. "It is changing. Or clarifying. Now there are tribal wars everywhere. 'Ethnic cleansing' has become a slogan around the world. That can't be denied."

"And you're not one to go with the flow?"

"Never have been."

"You called her Princess Annie Maggie?"

"What's that got to do with what we're talking about?"

"Something." Jack looked through the side window. "I think it has something to do with it. At least at one point in your life you accepted a hierarchical structure."

o◦◦○○○○◦◦◦○○

"Oh, I see. You think you've got me."

"Haven't I?" Jack asked.

Fletch said, *"Oi vey!"*

"Oi vey?" Jack said.

Softly, Jack had been playing the guitar and singing "Ol' Black Joe."

Going through the main square of Tolliver, Alabama, Fletch swerved the station wagon and stopped next to the curb.

Carrie was approaching them in the truck.

She parked against the curb on her side of the road.

Leary was still in the pen in the back of the truck.

Getting out of the station wagon, Fletch crossed the road to her.

"What in hell?" he asked.

"Fletch," Carrie said through the truck window, "have you ever heard the expression 'I couldn't get arrested'?"

"What happened? What are you doing here?"

"I got to the intersection at nine o'clock, on the dot. I pumped the accelerator, making the truck jerk so the jerk on the back would think we had engine trouble. I stopped. Fletch, there were no cops there! Not sign one of them. I got out, put the hood up, fiddled around with the engine. The goon in back was trying to climb over the cab's rooftop to help me. The calf bull kept buttin' him back. I had no choice but to slam down the hood and get going again."

"You didn't even go through a roadblock?"

"I never saw a cop anywhere. Not one. All the way here. I even sped. Went through stop signs. I tell you, man, I couldn't even get arrested. Do you think all the cops in two states have gone fishin'?"

"I doubt they'd catch any fish, either."

"I figured the best thing to do was come here. I've driven around the square four times, waiting for you. Tolliver doesn't seem to have even a traffic cop! Not even a school crossing guard!"

"My God, I'm sorry. I never meant to put you at risk for such a long time."

"I'm fine." Carrie indicated the back of the truck with her thumb. "Better than he is."

Fletch went to the back of the truck. "Hello, Leary. Have a nice ride?"

Leary was a mess. The calf bull had knocked out two of Leary's teeth. His eyes were blackened and swollen. His face was cut. There was a deep gash on his bare left shoulder. He was covered with dung.

His skin was painfully burned, as red as the setting sun. On top of the sunburn, Leary had dozens of tick bites.

Through his swollen lips, Leary said, "I'm firsty."

Fletch could not help a twinge of compassion for him.

The bull calf was no worse for his experience.

Carrie said, "He's crisped up pretty good."

Fletch had returned to the cab's window. "Beat up pretty good, too. Jack and Kriegel have been complaining of being thirsty all the way down."

Carrie smiled. "Bless their hearts."

"I guess you have to come with us now. Damn, I didn't mean this to happen. What happened to the sheriff? I couldn't have been more clear with him. How could he let you get by?"

oⓒoooⓒoooⓒo

"I don't know. Surprised me, too."

"Well, I guess you have to follow us."

"To the encampment?"

"Hey!" Leary shouted at him. "I'm firsty."

"Oh, shut up!" Fletch said. "Are you a tough guy, or not?"

"Tough guy," Leary confirmed.

"So." Fletch sighed. "Turn around and follow us."

"Okay."

"Carrie . . ."

"What?"

"You did do what you said you were going to do, didn't you? You did go to that intersection. I mean, you didn't come here because you were worried about me, or anything, did you?"

"Shoot no." She smiled. "I've seen too much of these villains as it is."

"I can't understand what happened to the sheriff."

"Best-laid plans," Carrie said, "often get screwed up."

"Yeah. But I'm not sure we can take care of both of us. Bringing a woman, you, into a camp full of psychotic males . . . When we get there, you watch your mouth, will you?"

"Why, I'll be as quiet as a church mouse while the collection plate is being passed."

"Nothing you say can change these fools, you know."

"Only thing they need," Carrie said, "is shootin'."

"Let's not start anything, all right?"

Carrie stuck her jaw out. "I won't if they don't."

Back across the road, Fletch opened the door to the front passenger seat. "You drive," he said to

Jack. "I'm not about to pass myself off as one of your merry band."

Scooting across the seat, Jack asked, "Do you know how to get to this encampment?"

"Sure." Fletch closed the door. "You know stupid people can't keep secrets."

Watching Carrie through the rearview mirror pull the truck up behind them, Jack said, "I was pretty sure you didn't mean Carrie to meet us here."

Fletch said nothing.

oᴼooᴼooᴼo

chapter 11

Fletch said to Carrie, "Welcome to Sherwood Forest."

"Yeah," Carrie said. "Where's the Sheriff of Nottingham when you need him?"

There were many strange-looking men standing around. For the most part they wore army camouflage pants and shirts. Many wore wide belts with holstered knives and handguns hanging from them. Some were overbuilt, some overly fat, many short and runty, many with their heads shaved, faces scarred by acne or cuts, several showing damage wrought by alcohol and other drugs, teeth missing, noses broken, peculiarly intense eyes, one with an ear missing. A few held semiautomatic weapons carelessly.

One shirtless citizen was as big as Leary.

"These are the racially superior?" Carrie asked.

Fletch said, "Hush your mouth, girl."

"They look like they were scraped off a tavern floor."

The men gathered around the back door of the station wagon.

Kriegel had waited for Jack to open the back door for him.

The Reverend Doctor Kris Kriegel stepped out of the back door of the station wagon like the Empress Catherine alighting from her golden coach.

He raised his arms. "I have come!"

Carrie muttered, "He wishes he had."

All the men standing around raised their right arms in stiff salute, except one, who raised his left arm.

There had been three men with semiautomatic weapons at the entrance to the encampment.

In a clipped voice, Jack had identified himself to them as "Lieutenant Faoni," Kriegel as "Commandant Kriegel," and told them Carrie and Leary in the truck behind them were part of the expected party.

"Who are you?" one of the men asked Fletch.

"Siegfried," Fletch said.

Jack said, "Code name: Siegfried."

They drove along a dirt road twisting through a thick forest.

Halfway along the road, another man stood with a semiautomatic weapon. He gave them a hard-eyed stare as they passed.

The encampment itself was a clearing of pasture gone to seed. In the most central place was a log cab-

o◯ooo◯ooo◯o

in with a fieldstone chimney, roofed front porch. At odd angles to each other were structures Fletch recognized as originally designed as carports: aluminum roofs held up by black poles in uneven cement floors. A few had their tarpaulin sides lowered, to keep out sun, rain, or eyes. Also at odd angles were several house trailers which had seen better days. Tipped on uneven cement blocks, their blue, white, gray, brown sides were sun-blistered. Recreational vehicles and smaller campers were parked helter-skelter throughout the clearing. At the edge of the woods around the clearing were many Porta Potties. In the midday heat, the smell from them permeated the camp.

The place looked like a wacky seven-year-old boy's idea of heaven.

More or less in the center of the clearing was a flagpole.

The flag hanging from it was not the flag of the United States of America.

It was not the flag of the Confederacy.

It was not the flag of the state of Alabama.

It was a flag with a red field. The black symbols on it each looked like a chicken's footprint.

"Listen to them," Carrie said. The men gathered around Kriegel were talking to him, to each other, in tones that sounded more tight, abrupt, angry than anything else. "There isn't one Southerner among them."

Fletch listened. "You're right."

"Why don't these boys stay home? Why don't they shit in their own beds?"

From the log cabin marched a middle-aged man.

o◯oo◯oo◯o

He was dressed in a brown uniform with patches featuring the chicken footprints on collar tabs and shoulders. His wide belt held in his sizable gut to a size forty-four. From it dangled a holstered six-shooter. In the sunlight, as he crossed the clearing, his hair was brassy.

Carrie snorted. "He must have gotten that dye job at the county fair!"

The man was followed by another similarly uniformed young man, a teenaged boy, carrying a clipboard.

"Firsty!" From his pen on the back of the truck, Leary pulled himself up on the bars. He had realized the truck had stopped moving. "Let me out!"

Fletch said to Leary: "Say 'please.' "

"Fuck you," Leary said.

The men parted for the neatly uniformed man. Standing before Kriegel, the man stood at attention. He tried to click the heels of his soft combat boots together. He gave the stiff-armed salute.

He introduced himself as Commandant Wolfe.

In a most languid manner, Kriegel returned the salute.

There were introductions all around. Right arms snapped up one by one.

"Can't they go to the Porta Potties without permission?" Carrie asked.

Kriegel and Wolfe drew closer together. Everyone began to look at Carrie and Fletch. Kriegel said, "Brunnehilde! . . . Siegfried! . . . Good for us to have them here . . . "

Fletch said, "Oh, Thor!"

As the two commandants walked toward the log

cabin, Jack approached Carrie and Fletch.

Carrie was looking at the calf bull on the back of the truck. "We have to get him in the shade, Fletch. Get him some water."

"Yes." The bull calf didn't need to say "please." He had done a good morning's work. Fletch said to Jack, "Help me lift the gate, will you? I think this bull calf has had just about enough of Leary's company."

Together they lifted the rear section of the pen.

Head and shoulders first, Leary crawled under the gate. He tripped on the truck's tailgate and landed facedown on the ground. He laughed.

As Jack and Fletch refitted the rear section of the cattle pen, Leary got up.

With a rumbling giggle he bounded over to the only man there who was as big as he was.

Laughing, he smashed his forehead into the forehead of the other man.

He knocked himself unconscious.

The men watched him collapse onto the ground. They looked at him with only a modicum of curiosity.

Leaving Leary as he was, continuing to broil in the sun, they wandered off.

Carrie started the truck. She began backing it between house trailers toward the shade of the woods.

Jack said to Fletch, "What are your plans?"

"I'm not sure," Fletch said.

"Are you going? Or do you mean to stay?"

Fletch hesitated. "I have some responsibility here. I helped you fools escape."

∞◯∞◯∞◯∞

Jack squinted at him. His smile was tight. "You mean to stay long enough to see what we're doing, and why, the purpose of all this, and then turn us in?"

"Something like that," Fletch said. "It's been interesting so far."

Then Jack's smile was genuine. "You saw that turning us in immediately would serve no purpose?"

"You let me see you had an objective," Fletch said. "You made me wonder what it was."

Jack laughed. "You took the bait."

"Yeah. I took the bait. You meant me to. So I did."

"Yes," Jack said. "I was hoping you would."

"Clearly you did. You didn't come cross-country to my house for my help. You would have been better off without it. You could have been here yesterday."

"That's for sure. With easy access to Moreno's money."

"You came to my house to involve me."

"So far, it's worked out pretty well." Jack stuck his finger against Fletch's solar plexus. "Siegfried."

"Enough of that shit."

Jack took a wad of bills out of his shorts pocket. "Two thousand dollars. Commandant Wolfe gave it to me. He wants me to rebuild the sound system."

"What sound system?"

"There will be speeches this evening. Will you drive me into Huntsville to get the equipment I need?"

"Carrie will have to come with us. Or go home."

"It would be better if she came with us."

○c○○○○○○○○○○○○

"Why?"

"Your theory. Cops look more closely at two men than they would two men and a woman."

"I guess so."

"I'll go check it out," Jack said. "See what we need. I'll be right back. After I get something to drink. After I get a whole lot to drink."

"Sure," Fletch said. "We'll do lunch."

"Fletch, there are women and children down there. Little children! Babies! In that big, filthy trailer."

Fletch had wandered down to where Carrie had parked the truck.

Somehow she had gotten a big plastic tub onto the back of the truck, upside right. While the bull calf slobbered up the water, she poured more from a bucket through the rails of the pen.

"The children are filthy, Fletch. Dirty diapers everywhere. The trailer stinks. I think they're hungry. The women seem half out of it. What are we going to do?"

"We're going into Huntsville," Fletch said. "With Jack. Unless you'd rather take the truck and go home. I rather you would."

"I can't leave these children here. There's a girl down there stuffing uncooked hamburger into a toothless baby's mouth!"

"Well, you know," Fletch said. "In this context. Women and children . . . "

"We've got to get them some baby food. Milk. Diapers. Soap. If we get them some soap, is there any way they can wash their clothes?"

"I don't know."

o◯ooＯoo◯o

"I'm going with you," Carrie said. "And I'm coming back."

"That's odd." Carrie, in the middle front seat of the station wagon, craned to look over Fletch's shoulder. Fletch driving, they were just entering the long wooded driveway out of the encampment. "A forest-green four-door Saturn with Tennessee license plates."

"What's odd about that?" Fletch, too, turned to look but could see nothing but the woods. "You finally found a car with Southern plates?"

"Francie drives a forest-green Saturn."

"Francie who?"

"Joe Rogers's wife."

Jack sat to Carrie's right.

"Sheriff Joe Rogers?" Fletch asked.

"Yeah," Carrie said.

Fletch said, "Must be a coincidence."

"Must be," Carrie said.

chapter 12

"Hello, Andy. How's your head bone?"

"Feels like less a bone, thank you, Mister Fletcher, more like a head. I swear, I got a good case of sound poisoning last night."

"I suppose it's possible. First, please tell me about the 'seismic disturbance' in California. I still haven't heard any news."

"Cable is one thing, Mister Fletcher; I've heard your excuses for not watching GCN, but don't you even have a radio down on that farm? A wireless? Are you too far from town to pick up the tom-toms?"

"Yes, Andy, we have radios. I just haven't had the chance all morning to work the pedals to pump one up. They're antique radios anyway. They only pick up Rudy Vallee and news of World War Two."

Fletch sat in the station wagon in the sun-drenched parking lot of a shopping mall in Huntsville, Alabama.

The trip there from the encampment had been quiet. Carrie had sat in the front seat between Fletch and Jack.

Fletch had begun, once they had left the dust of the encampment behind them, by asking Jack, "Did you go to school, do all sorts of good things? Sports?"

"Oh, sure."

"Where did you go to school?"

"Bloomington. Chicago. Boston."

"Boston? Why Boston?"

"Why not Boston?"

Over the ignored condition of the babies, children, women Carrie had discovered at the encampment, their hunger, their filth, what she believed she identified as evidences of physical abuse, her fury emanated as palpably from her as would a strong odor. She had difficulty even looking at Jack. Clearly, she had no interest in anything he had to say.

Sensing this, Jack had no interest in talking.

Fletch hummed "What a swell party this is . . . "

As soon as Fletch stopped the car in the shopping mall's parking lot, Jack was out the door headed for an electronics store. Separately, Carrie headed for a supermarket.

Fletch took the cellular phone from under the car seat and pressed in Andy Cyst's office phone number at Global Cable News in Virginia.

"The California earthquakes," Andy mused, as if asked to discuss something that had happened in sixteenth-century France. "Considerable."

"Considerable what? Damage?"

"Yes. No estimates yet. Covered a wide area along the southern coast. Power lines, water lines disturbed, some fires, a small bridge fell in, no major buildings collapsed, although many will have to be inspected before being occupied again, two deaths reported so far. Two aftershocks reported. Geologists are saying there is no more to worry about than there was before. That's reassuring, isn't it? The governor of California has issued a statement reminding people that most of California is not affected by earthquakes at all. I suspect that bit was written for him by the Chamber of Commerce goaded by amusement park operators."

"That's called a positive spin."

"Anyway, the California earthquake story has knocked out much interest in your prison escapees story. Ordinarily, that story would be getting a big play. But, as it is, there's almost no coverage of it."

"Why would it have been getting a big play in particular?"

"Because of who one of them is. By the way, I was wrong. There were three escapees."

"Three?"

"Yes. Kris Kriegel, the most interesting, who would be drawing the most attention, if it weren't for the California earthquakes, fifty-three years old, a native of South Africa, son of once-wealthy landowners with banking interests. He has his doctor of philosophy degree in cultural anthropology from the University of Warsaw, Poland. In South Africa,

oᴄ◯ooᴄ◯ooᴄ◯o

he was an apartheid activist, and a leader of the neo-Nazi movement there. He is suspected as one of the originators of the plan to instigate warfare among the tribes. He was present, in a neo-Nazi uniform, at the so-called 'trod-through' in Soweto, when, as you remember, seventy-two blacks—men, women, and children—were massacred by a white gang for which the old South African government denied all responsibility, and, damn their eyes, knowledge."

"Yes."

"Immediately thereafter, Kriegel spent some years based in Poland, without known employment, with frequent trips to Germany, France, and England. After that big riot in Munich on the anniversary of Kristallnacht, if you remember, in which forty-eight people—Jews, Slavs, homosexuals—were stabbed and beaten to death randomly in the streets, nine Pakistanis were burned to death in their boardinghouse, Kriegel came to this country, essentially as a fugitive from justice. The German government wanted to 'interview' him regarding these murders. Almost immediately after his arrival in this country he was apprehended, indicted, tried, found guilty, and sentenced for murder in the second degree of a prostitute in his hotel room. I guess in the throes of some sort of sexual whatever, maybe frustration, he strangled her to death. Incidentally, she was a black woman."

"You're making me sick."

"And Kris Kriegel seems like such a friendly name. Doesn't it? Kris Kringle. Sleigh bells ring, all that."

oℂ○○○ℂ○○○ℂ○

"Roasting . . . "

"In prison, incidentally, Kriegel has continued his old ways. He took to calling himself 'Reverend' and preaching 'ethnic cleansing,' racism, I guess, the same old ordure of the anal retentive. There have been two race riots in the federal penitentiary at Tomaston, Kentucky, in the last five months."

"I didn't know that."

"The prison system tries not to give such incidents much PR. A black guard was murdered in one. He was hung upside down until dead."

Sitting in his car in the Alabama parking lot, his door open to catch a breeze, Fletch envisioned the pudgy, little man, gray hair standing out above his ears, the blue birthmark saddle over the bridge of his nose, whom he had seen mostly quietly asleep, sitting up, hands folded in his lap, like any grandfather dreaming up plans for his grandchildren and their friends.

He had plans for the children, all right.

"Juan Moreno, thirty-eight years old, a citizen of Colombia," Andy Cyst droned on, "believed to be a member of the Medellin drug cartel. It is believed Juan Moreno is not his real name. Mostly, it says here, his job was to buy airplanes and boats for smuggling, and to establish landing situations in this country. He was caught driving an ambulance loaded with cocaine in east Texas. The uniformed driver of the ambulance was dead on the gurney in back. He had bled to death from the hole made by a screwdriver through his throat. Moreno was not found guilty of his murder, but of just about everything else. A full briefcase of bankbooks, real estate deeds, other documentation was found in the front seat of the ambulance with him. Various names were on the documents, but all the significant signatures were in his handwriting."

And Fletch thought of "Moreno," his throat swollen, his body bloating, twisted among the debris in the gully, snake-bitten, drowned, blank brown eyes staring up at a blank blue sky.

Fletch said, "Moreno has been found, right?"

"No."

"No?"

"No report of it. And our last report is twenty minutes old."

"Oh, boy." Tiredness flowed against Fletch like a warm breeze.

"John Leary," Andy Cyst said. "He almost doesn't exist as a person. He's just a rap sheet. He's almost never been free. Thirty-two years old. He has been in institutions since he was eight years old. He was first institutionalized as an 'unruly child.'"

"At age eight?"

"There is a notation here that he is a very large and physically dangerous person."

"Even at age eight no one could handle him?"

"While waiting for Juvenile Court in Pennsylvania to dispose of him, as it were, he fractured the skull of a child psychologist assigned to test him. Wouldn't you call that just a bit 'unruly' of an eight-year-old child?"

"Pesky."

"His rap sheet is amazing. The authorities would put him out in foster care, and he would attack someone. They'd institutionalize him, and he'd attack

oc○oo○ooo○o

someone. A great one for inflicting bodily harm."

"Antisocial."

"Psychotic. 'Armed robbery, armed robbery, armed robbery,' " Andy read. " 'General mayhem, assault, assault, assault. Arson. Assault upon an officer of the law.' His last conviction was for kidnapping a teenaged girl, transporting her across state lines for immoral purposes, keeping her captive for immoral purposes, multiple rapes, and slavery. What does 'slavery' mean?"

"He tried to sell her in a bar. A pool hall or something."

"Oh, you do know something?"

"Of course. Why do you think I need to know more?"

"Mister Fletcher, you haven't come across these people, have you? I mean, do you know where they are?"

"I'll tell you one thing," Fletch said.

"What's that?"

"Leary hasn't much future as a matador, either. Even a bull he attacks from the wrong end. I remain puzzled. You're only telling me about three escapees, Andy. The local sheriff said there were four."

"There are only three."

"Isn't there another name on the printout you're reading?"

"I've read you everything I have. There are three escapees: Kriegel, Moreno, Leary. This isn't a new story now. It's almost twenty-four hours old. These are the facts. There were only three escapees from the federal penitentiary at Tomaston, Mister Fletcher."

oᴏⒸᴏᴏᴏⒸᴏᴏᴏⒸᴏ

"I don't get it. Why did the sheriff say four? He even had a name."

"You know better than I, news stories at first are often garbled."

"Yeah, but."

"I will say that this printout I'm reading from looks like it might have had a deletion."

"What do you mean?"

"There's a big space between Moreno and Leary. It looks like something was deleted and the space wasn't closed up. Probably just some kind of a human error."

Fletch said, "Probably."

"Regarding Ms. Crystal Faoni," Andy said. He recited to Fletch her age, home address in Bloomington, Indiana, office address, the call letters and addresses of the five radio stations she owns around the state, the fact that she was never known to have married, has one son, John Faoni, who has graduated from Northwestern University, attended Boston University, currently is traveling in Greece; Ms. Faoni has no criminal record, a perfect credit record, and currently is spending time at a health spa in Wisconsin.

The sunlight glared on and through the windshield of the station wagon. Fletch closed his eyes. He left them closed.

Greece.

"I called her home," Andy Cyst said. "Someone working for a cleaning service answered. Her office said she has gone to this health spa for two weeks. She is not to be disturbed under any circumstances. Her secretary said Ms. Faoni is concentrating on a weight-loss program that involves meditation. What meditation?" Andy asked. "Not thinking about hunger and food is called meditation now?"

"Omm," Fletch said, eyes still closed. "Think yourself to a slimmer you."

"She must be a shapely woman, to care this much about her weight."

"She is shapely," Fletch agreed.

"The secretary did not want to give me the name and number of the health spa, but I used my great charm, and won her over. She knew the staff at the health spa would block me anyway. They did. Ms. Faoni is not to be disturbed. She is concentrating. Meditating. Whatever."

"Where is it?"

"It's called Blythe Spirit."

"No."

"In a place called Forward, Wisconsin."

"America," Fletch said.

"About a hundred miles from Chicago."

"Sounds like a story, Andy."

"What?"

"An interesting feature story for GCN." Fletch opened his eyes. "I might want a crew to go there with me."

"Anything you say, Mister Fletcher. You're GCN's only consulting/contributing editor without a cable hookup."

"It keeps me fresh."

"Actually, I believe it does. Is there anything else you need for now?"

"Nothing you can do for me. Thanks, Andy."

"A su órdenes, señor."

oᕗ○○ᕗ○○○ᕗo

*   *   *

Fletch sat a long moment, half in, half out of the car, dead telephone in hand.

Even though dressed just in cotton shorts and shirt, he was soaked with sweat. Always he had noticed builders in this area of the South never left trees, or any source of shade, in their parking lots. Trees are pretty, give shade, lessen the need for air-conditioning, but golly gee, take up as much as a square foot of ground space.

Instead of thinking about all that perplexed him, Fletch sat in the sun thinking of trees.

Slowly, he pressed Alston Chambers's office number into the telephone's panel.

The secretary put him right through.

"You guys are okay?" Fletch asked.

"The first so-called aftershock broke my whole shelf of Steuben glass," Alston said. "Every piece of it. Including my best golf trophy."

"Why would a Californian have Steuben glass on a shelf?" Fletch asked.

"Where was I supposed to put it?" Alston nearly shouted. "Between two mattresses on a gimbal table?"

"Sounds good."

"Busted pipes. I had to shave with Apollonaris."

"Sorry. Did it tickle?"

"This bouncin' around out here is gettin' tiresome, Fletch."

"I'm sure it is."

"People drive along looking at the tops of buildings and they run smack into each other. From one thing and another, there's glass all over the streets out here."

"There's an idea."

"What?"

"Go into the glass business."

"Are you still in the smokehouse?"

"I wish I were. I'm in a very hot parking lot."

"You and Carrie all right?"

"Fine."

"Where's your so-called son?"

"In Greece."

"What?"

"Never mind. I'm hot and tired. Sun-dazed. Nothing makes any sense."

"You didn't make any sense last time you called, either."

"What do you mean?"

"There is a Crystal Faoni extant. And at the moment she is *incommunicado* at a place called Blathering Spooks or something in some place called Up-and-At-'Em, Wisconsin, or somewhere. I've got it right here."

"That's okay. I've got it, too. When I called you this morning, I couldn't get through. Would you believe the telephone company has recorded its message notifying callers of your seismic disturbances?"

"But everything else you said was crazy. Only three men escaped from Tomaston Prison. Their names are Moreno, Leary, and Kriegel. No Faoni."

"Alston, are you sure?"

"Fletch, I talked with the Attorney General of the state of Kentucky. I talked with the warden of Tomaston Prison. I talked with the Justice Depart-

∘◗∘∘◗∘∘◗∘

ment in Washington, D.C. No Faoni."

"I don't understand."

"There never has been a Faoni."

"What?"

"The federal penitentiary in Tomaston, Kentucky, did not, and never has had an inmate named Faoni."

"John Fletcher—"

"Not John Fletcher Faoni, not Alexander Faoni, not Betty Boop Faoni. I have just checked the entire federal penal system. There never has been an inmate named John Fletcher Faoni."

I'm being used, Fletch said to himself. *I knew it. I am being involved in something. . . . But by whom? For what reason? This kid knows about me things only Crystal knows . . . our tumbling out of the shower . . . Kriegel recognized a physical similarity. . . . Carrie said we are similar. . . . John Fletcher Faoni has not been a prisoner. . . . He is in Greece. . . .*

Alston asked, "Are you fantasizing up a son in your dotage? A big one? One you don't have to burp?"

Dragging two loaded shopping carts behind him, Jack was crossing the parking lot toward Fletch.

Heat waves from the noonday sun were rising from the pavement in the parking lot.

In fact, Jack was an apparition shimmering in the heat waves like a moving figure in a fun house mirror.

"A fantasy," Fletch said. "Maybe a fantasy."

"Fletch, are you all right?"

"I've got to hang up, Alston. Hide the phone."

"Hide the phone?"

Fletch hung up.

And hid the phone.

o○○○◯○○○o

* * *

As soon as Jack loaded his electronic equipment into the back of the station wagon, Carrie appeared with bundles and bundles of milk, cereals, baby food, diapers, soap, cleaning fluids, brushes, mops . . .

The three of them sat as before in the car.

Almost perfectly silently.

Fletch asked, "Lunch, anyone?"

"Fast food," Carrie said. "In the car. I've got to get back." Slowly, with jaw jutting, she looked up from Jack's legs to his waist to his chest to his face. "Before I'm guilty of child abuse, too."

"If that's the case," Jack said, "we have to stop at a drugstore, too."

"What for?" Carrie still stared at his profile. "You run out of mean pills?"

"Concentrated salt," Jack said. "To sprinkle on baked ham."

"What do you want to stop for?" Fletch asked.

"Earplugs."

Carrie said, "Now there's a good idea. Get some for us, too."

"I will."

As the car rolled forward, Jack slid the tips of the fingers of his right hand down his left forearm. He said, "I'm hardly sweating at all. Must be all that salt I had for breakfast." Jack looked at Fletch and Carrie. He smiled broadly. "You guys seem to be sweating a whole lot!"

In fact, they were.

o⊂OooᗑOOⵔo

chapter 13

"Sonsabitches. Damned bastards. I hate to accept their food."

In the reclined driver's seat of the station wagon, Fletch had slept most of the afternoon. He awoke when Carrie opened the door and got into the front passenger seat.

The sun had lowered considerably, but not the temperature.

Carrie handed Fletch a plastic bowl of chili, a plastic spoon, and a can of soda. She had her own bowl of chili and can of soda.

"Then don't," Fletch said. "Let's not eat their food."

"I have to. I'm starving," she said. "Anyway, I brought enough food into this place to get something in return." She looked like she had been ridden hard and put up wet. She tasted her chili. "Yee! It tastes like chopped horned toads and ketchup! These foreigners don't even know how to make respectable chili!"

Before sleeping, Fletch had parked the station wagon in the shade of the trees not far from his truck, but facing away from the center of the encampment. He was overlooking three rotting trailers around which there were women and children moving slowly if at all in the heat.

He and Carrie had brought the bags of groceries and cleaning materials down to the trailers. Indeed, close up, the women and children did look malnourished. They were listless. Their clothes and their skin were ingrained with dirt. Both the women and children had enough bruises to satisfy Fletch that at least this part of the encampment was ruled by iron fists and steel-toed boots.

A few of the boy children were dressed in little camouflage suits and combat boots. One six-year-old boy was fully dressed in a uniform similar to that worn by Commandant Wolfe, even to the chicken-footprint insignias.

The girl children and women were dressed in cotton shifts thinned by wear. Many were barefoot.

He thought if he slept lightly in the station wagon he could keep a cat's eye on Carrie as she tried to organize feeding-cleaning-and-washing brigades at the trailers. Surely a yell from her would awaken him no matter how soundly he slept.

Fletch did not even taste his chili.

"Guess what happened?" Carrie asked.

○⬤○○○⬤○○○⬤○

"Tell me."

"Three of these jerks came down to the trailers. At first they just stood and stared at me. Pulling from beer cans and whiskey bottles. Eyes bulging, you know? Pants bulging. I've seen it before."

"Why didn't you wake me up?"

"No need to. They came closer. Began making remarks. You know."

"About you?"

"Sure. They were spread out, one on each side, one in the middle, making a triangle, so I couldn't have gotten off the porch of the trailer. Fletch, I really believe they would have done it right there, in front of the women and children. You know? Put me in my place."

"Carrie!"

"Calm down. Guess who showed up and smashed two of their heads together and kicked the third one's ass so hard I declare he fractured his tailbone."

"Jack."

"No. Leary."

"Uh?"

"Leary. He roared at them, 'Leave my lady alone! She's nice to me! She's my friend!'" Carrie giggled.

Cross-legged, Leary sat near them in the shade. He was scooping chili from a huge plastic bowl with his fingers. Most of it made it into his mouth.

From his sharing the cattle pen on the back of the truck with a bull calf all the way down from the farm, his mouth—lips beaten, missing teeth—should have been too sore to take in food. The areas around his eyes were swollen and purple. The gash on his

oⓄooⓄooⓄo

shoulder had not been cleaned any more than the rest of him. The manure on his overalls and in his hair had dried.

Still shirtless in the split overalls, his skin looked painfully red from sunburn. He was covered with festering tick bites.

"We sure have been nice to him," Fletch drawled.

"We surely have."

"I guess he thinks so. Nicer than anybody else, I guess. For the rest of the afternoon he has stayed within three or four meters of me. I swanee, I'm safer here than at a Daughters of the American Revolution convention!"

Fletch said, "Glad he appreciates all we've done for him."

"There's something else I must tell you."

"Isn't attempted gang rape enough?"

"I snuck over for a peek at the license plate of that forest-green Saturn."

Fletch shrugged. "Oh?"

"Fletch, the license plate is from our county."

Even without having tasted the chili, Fletch felt a very unpleasant sensation in his belly. "Carrie, you and I both know Sheriff Joe Rogers. I've been huntin' and fishin' with him. He's been to the farm more often than the Jehovah's Witnesses. Never by word or deed has he expressed anything racist I've noticed."

"Only an ignoramus would, in front of you."

Again, Fletch said, "It must be a coincidence. There must be more than one green Saturn in the county."

Carrie said, "I'm pretty sure it's Francie's car."

oᴄ◯ooᴄ◯ooᴄ◯o

Quietly, Fletch said, "I sincerely hope it isn't."

Carrie said, "That makes two of us, bubba."

"Carrie, why don't you climb into the truck and take yourself home?"

"What are you doin' here?"

"Watching. Listening. Thinking."

"You think you're at a railroad crossing, or something?"

"We know this young man is a liar."

"We do?"

"While you and Jack were shopping I stayed in the car and used the phone."

"I guessed as much."

Fletch said, "There was no inmate in the federal penitentiary at Tomaston, Kentucky, or in any federal penitentiary, named Faoni. Never has been."

Carrie swallowed the last spoonful of chili out of her bowl. "Faoni was stenciled on his shirt. So were the words 'Federal Penitentiary Tomaston.'"

"I know. Anybody can stencil anything on clothes."

"So this kid wasn't in prison?"

"This kid must have been. How else would he know and have the trust of Kriegel, Leary. . . . But if he was in prison, his name isn't Faoni."

"So this kid isn't your son."

"The question remains on the floor, as the parliamentarian said, considering the chair."

"Is there a John Fletcher Faoni? You think he may have just known Crystal, and he's making this whole thing up?"

"There is a John Fletcher Faoni. Son of Crystal Faoni. And he did go to school in Bloomington, Chicago, and Boston."

oᴄ◌◌◌◌◌ᴏ

"So?"

"According to his mother's secretary, John Fletcher Faoni is spending the summer in Greece."

"In Greece," Carrie repeated. "Well, this surely isn't Greece."

"No. It isn't."

"It's not even on the way to Greece, from anywhere much."

"No. So we know this kid lies. If he lies about one thing, why not lie about everything? There's no point in asking a liar for the truth, is there? I just have to cool it. Watch, wait, and listen. Why is he lying? Who is he? What's his purpose?"

"You didn't speak to Crystal herself?"

"No. She's out of pocket. *Incommunicado* on some sort of a fat farm. Well, it's more than that: I guess it's a place for people with serious food addictions. Andy Cyst did not succeed in getting through to her."

Carrie said, "We're all addicted to food."

"There is a food addiction that is life-threatening."

"Wow. Humans sure go awry easy. I was addicted to ice, once."

"You needed iron. This young man said he shot at a cop. Is it true? This young man said he was in prison for attempted murder. Is it true? This young man says his name is John Fletcher Faoni. Not all of the above can be true."

"This kid could be as crazy as a groundhog on ice."

"True."

"It's a fact that he's hangin' out with these racists."

o⌒oooᴑooo⌒o

"That's why we're here. Who is he? What is he? What does he want from me?"

"He's the self-styled 'lieutenant' of the murdering self-styled leader of a self-styled international hate group."

"As some journalists would put it, 'He sure appears to be goin' with this particular flow.'"

"I suspect it's not every man's dream to discover his son is a cop-killing, escaped convict, racist, hate-group organizer."

"It's not a dream that has ever occurred to me."

"So if he's such a jerk, even if he is your kid, why should you care enough to stay here?"

"If I leave now I might lose track of him forever. Then I'll never know the truth."

"Maybe you won't want to know the truth."

"I always want to know the truth."

"The truth can make you a prisoner, Fletch."

"Carrie, I want you to go home."

"No, sir."

"Why not?"

"'Cause if I go I'll be worried to death about you."

"I've been in worse situations."

"If I stay, I'm pretty sure you'll get us both out in time."

"In time for what?"

Carrie was looking at the dark hills surrounding the encampment. "This is a foreboding place."

Fletch said, "Speak of the specter."

Jack was under the trees coming toward them. From one hand dangled headphones on short wires.

"Don't speak of ghosts to me." Carrie leaned for-

ward in her car seat and watched Jack approach.
"The kid walks like you."

"Yeah. He puts one foot in front of the other. Don't
see just what you want to see, miss."

"His hips and shoulders don't move when he walks.
Just his legs."

"Sure," Fletch muttered. "As evidence, that's not
exactly equal to a DNA test, is it?"

The station wagon's front doors were open.

"Enjoyin' yourselves?" Jack asked.

"Yes," Fletch answered. "But nothing else."

"Don't like your chili?" He looked at the untouched
chili in Fletch's bowl.

"You can have it." Fletch handed it to him.

Jack put the earphones on Fletch's lap.

"What did your cook season it with?" Carrie asked.
"Dried ragweed?"

Jack tasted it. "Yuck!"

Carrie said to Fletch, "The boy knows bad chili
when he tastes it. Must have some sense."

"What are the earphones for?" Fletch asked.

"You." Jack was eating the chili. "You all." He
took two sets of earplugs from the pocket of his
shorts and put them in Fletch's hand. "Put these
in your ears. When you see me put my headphones on, you both put yours on. And leave them
on until I take mine off. Earplugs and headphones."

"Why?"

"Kriegel's about to give a speech."

"Give me those ear-stoppers," Carrie said.

Jack said, "I fixed the sound system."

Fletch said, "I don't get it."

∞○∞○○∞

Commandant Wolfe was striding toward them.

Jack said, "Wear your ear-stoppers."

Wolfe stood at attention near the open car door. Jack backed up. He continued to eat his chili. "I am Commandant Wolfe!"

"I'm Shalom Aleichem." Fletch stuck his thumb toward Carrie. "This is Golda Meir, as a girl."

"Doctor Kriegel has warned me of your sense of humor, Mister Fletcher."

Fletch said, "It is tolerable."

"You may make these jokes, Mister Fletcher, but you and your lady are what you are and you can be nothing else."

"Come again?"

"You will see. Those of you who believe in one world, the brotherhood of races, miscegenation, quickly will change your minds when there is only one deer left in the forest. Quickly you will learn with which pack of dogs you run."

Carrie and Fletch looked at each other.

The Afro-American civil rights leader who recently had discussed matters with Fletch on the terrace behind the farmhouse at one point had burst into laughter and said, "Ah, Fletch! You're not going to give me that one-world crap, are you?"

In the car, Carrie lowered her head so Wolfe could see her. She barked. "Aarrf!"

Softly, Fletch said, "Since the beginning of time, a few have taken the fact of economic competition, no matter how great the resources, and used it to create hatred and violence to satisfy their own greed."

"Aarrf!" Carrie nodded in agreement.

o○oo○oo○o

Fletch looked into Wolfe's eyes. "And that's no joke."

"Aarrf! Aarrf!" Carrie sat back. "Fletch, did I hear right? Did he call me a bitch?"

"So far, I don't think he's actually spoken to you. Or looked at you."

"Notify him I'm fixin' to bite his ankle."

Wolfe handed Jack a six-pack of condoms.

He also handed one to Fletch.

"I beg your pardon?" Fletch asked.

"Once used, please turn them in at headquarters. A clerk will label them properly."

"Our semen," Jack said to Fletch, "will be stored. And used."

"I beg your pardon?" Fletch asked.

"By artificial insemination," Jack said. "To continue and improve our race."

"Mister Fletcher." Commandant Wolfe still stood at attention. "You must agree all the wrong people are having children!"

"About your parents," Fletch said, "indeed I do agree."

Wolfe's cheeks colored. "Do this! It is your duty!"

He did a military about-face. Chin high, shoulders back, he marched away, up the slope, over rough ground.

"Well, I'll be Adam's uncle," Carrie said. "Did you ever?"

"No," Fletch answered.

Jack was watching Fletch.

"Here." Fletch handed the condoms to Carrie. "Give these to your friend Leary. Save the world a lot of trouble."

o○○o○○○o○○○○o

Empty chili bowl in one hand, with his other hand Jack tossed the pack of condoms into the air and caught it. "How can I object?" Jack said. "I am a result of selective breeding. Aren't I?"

chapter 14

There were between fifty and sixty men gathered in the middle of the encampment.

It was clear from their faces, the way they stood, talked, that many of these happy campers had ingested one form of intoxicant or another, or more than one form.

They were primed for firing.

Brush and old wood had been piled high at the other end of the central clearing. So there was to be a bonfire, Fletch surmised.

Among them stood a fat, bald man in a dirty white apron. He carried a metal ladle.

"That must be the chef," Carrie said. "I must ask him where he gets his ragweed."

A few women stood together at a distance from

the men. Babies and girl children were with them. Boy children stood among the men.

A microphone, speakers at a distance each side of it, had been placed at the top of the three steps on the porch of the log cabin.

Fletch and Carrie stood well away from the crowd of men, to the side, where they could see almost everything well.

At the front of the men, Jack was adjusting a camcorder on a tripod.

"My, my," Fletch said to Carrie. "This is being taped."

" 'Vanity, vanity,' " Carrie said. " 'All is vanity.' "

"More than that," Fletch said. "Like their predecessors, they are carefully documenting their own history."

"So later they can deny it, right?"

Commandant Wolfe came through the door of the log cabin onto the porch. He was followed by Commandant The Reverend Doctor Kris Kriegel. He was still dressed in the ill-fitting slacks and shirt Carrie had found in one of the farm's closets. The uniformed young man, still carrying the clipboard, was the last through the door.

Three times the men standing before the cabin raised their right arms in the stiff salute. Three times they shouted "Heil!"

Wolfe raised his eyes to the flag on the pole behind the men, raised his right arm, and said, "Heil!" only once, not loudly.

Fletch noticed that in this moment of concentrated rapture, Jack had taken the camcorder off the tripod.

⦿⦾∘⦾∘⦾∘⦾⦿

Crouched, he was videotaping the audience, moving back and forth.

Jack was recording every face.

At the microphone, Wolfe began to speak. There were a few sentences of greeting. He referred to his audience as *real men, real American men.* There was a joke about how surprised, upset their *Jewish employers* would be if they knew where these men were this night. Their *Jewish employers* wouldn't know whether to give their jobs to *the ass-licking niggers* or just sell out to *those yellow, slanty-eyed, Asian, pocket-sized, battery-operated calculators.*

Fletch watched Carrie.

Her mouth dropped open. Beneath her tan, her face drained of blood, turned white. Even her freckles receded, like stars when the moon appears. Her eyes widened and blazed blue.

She turned her face toward him. "Fletch . . . "

The skin around her eyes began to wrinkle.

"Don't say anything," Fletch said. "Don't cry."

As if in a nearly fainting condition, as if appealing to him, her fingertips brushed Fletch's forearm. "I can't stand this."

"I know."

"Why do they come here to do this, say these horrid things? The license plates on the vehicles . . . they're not from around here."

"They're everywhere now," Fletch said. "North, south, east, west." At last reckoning there were 346 groups such as this in the United States of America, up twenty-seven percent from the year before. "Great Britain, France, Germany, Poland, the Balkans, Russia. The Middle East. Africa. Ethnic cleansing.

Separatism." Fletch had guessed Kriegel had come to the United States to draw these groups together, and strengthen their ties with similar movements abroad.

Having been caught, tried, convicted, and sentenced for that "irrelevancy" in Washington surely must have frustrated him.

"The children." Carrie's eyes were wet with tears. "The babies."

"I know."

Carrie listened another minute.

Not hiding at all what she was doing, she then put the earplugs in her ears.

Encouraged by applause, whistles, shouts of *White rights!* Wolfe spoke on, and on, and on. There were references to those of African descent as *the mud people*. To those of Jewish descent as *the children of Satan*. To the United States government as *Z.O.G., just another Zionist organization.*

Not hearing much of anything of what Wolfe was saying, Carrie's shoulders relaxed somewhat. She folded her arms across her chest. She stared at the ground in front of her.

Her face remained pale.

Clearly Wolfe had studied the newsreels of Mussolini. He folded his arms high across his chest. Lips in a downward crescent, he nodded his head violently in affirmation of everything he said, every noise of approbation from his audience. He strutted back and forth to the microphone between each utterance, raising his feet like a rooster on a gossip bench.

Fletch remembered the overwhelming sadness he

oＯooＯooＯo

had felt once in East Africa when his friend Juma
had brought him and Fletch's then wife, Barbara,
to Shimoni, a huge cave at the edge of the Indian
Ocean. . . .

*. . . Fletch and Barbara did not know what
they were seeing. To them, Shimoni was a hard-
packed mud descent into darkness. Something,
not a sound, not a smell, something palpable
emanated from the cave.*

"Do you wish to enter?" Juma asked.

Fletch glanced at Barbara. "Why not?"

*"Going down is slippery." Juma looked at the
knapsack on Fletch's back.*

Fletch put the pack on the ground.

*"There are bats." Juma looked at Barbara's
hair.*

"It's a cave," Fletch said.

"Is it a big cave?" Barbara asked.

*"It goes along underground about twelve
miles," Juma said.*

"What am I feeling?" Fletch asked.

Juma nodded.

He led the way down the slippery slope.

*They stood in an enormous underground room,
partly lit by the light from the entrance. Barbara
remarked on the stalactites, then giggled at the
hollow sound of her voice.*

*Fletch noticed that all the rock, every square
centimeter of floor, all along the walls two meters
high, had been worn smooth. Even in imperfect
light, much of the stone looked polished.*

"What was this place used for?" Fletch asked.

oᴄ◌◌ᴏ◌◌◌ᴏ

A bat flew overhead.

"A warehouse," Juma said simply. "For human beings. A human warehouse. People who had been sold as slaves were jammed in here, to await the ships that took them away."

Only the slow drip of water somewhere in the cave punctuated the long, stunned silence.

When Barbara's face turned back toward them, toward the light, her cheeks glistened with tears.

"How afraid they must have been," she said.

Juma said, "For hundreds of years."

"The terror," Barbara said. "The utter despair."

Juma said, "The smell, the sweat, the shit of hundreds, maybe thousands of bodies. The crying that must have come from this cave, day and night, year after year."

The entrance to the cave was wide, but not so wide it could not be sealed by a few men with swords and guns, clubs and whips. The rear of the cave was total darkness. That damp, reeking, weeping darkness extending twelve miles underground, no way out from under the heaviness of the earth, however frantic, however intelligent, however energetic the effort, to light, to air, to food, back to their own realities, existences, their own loves, lives, expectations. . . .

There was only one way out of that cave: docile, enslaved.

"Did your ancestors buy slaves, do you think?"

"No," Fletch answered.

"I'm pretty sure not," said Barbara.

oOooOooOo

*Juma ran his bare foot over the smoothness
of the floor stone. "You see, that is how we must
think of things."*

"What do you mean?" Fletch asked.

*"I'm pretty sure my ancestors sold slaves. Do
you see? Which is worse—to buy people or to sell
them?"*

. . . So again Fletch stood with a woman who was
deeply shocked, deeply saddened, her cheeks glistening with tears in less than perfect light; he, saddened
before, saddened now, but now, half the world away,
also enraged at the ignorance of the many, the pur-
poseful ignorance of the few who manipulated such
ignorance for their own power-mongering, greedy
ends . . . enraged. . . .

To rousing cheers and chants of *White rights!
White rights!* Wolfe finished his speech and, arms
still folded high across his chest, stepped back.

Kriegel stepped forward to speak.

His voice was higher than Wolfe's. "I hereby name
this camp," he shrieked, "Camp Orania!"

The audience roared its approval.

Fletch doubted many, if any, in the audience knew
what Orania signified. In the wasteland of Karoo,
South Africa, Orania is the name of the headquarters
of the Afrikaner Resistance Movement.

Without doubt, Kriegel meant it as a great
compliment to the establishment of this camp in
Alabama.

"Hey." Fletch nudged Carrie. Having her attention, he nodded his head, indicating Jack.

Apparently leaving the camcorder on the tripod to

oc◯oo◯oo◯o

run itself, Jack had gone forward to a sound console on a bench just in front of the porch of the log cabin. He had put on his earphones. He was fiddling with some dials.

Fletch inserted his earplugs, concealing what he was doing no more than Carrie had. Then he put on his headphones. They were plugged into nothing. He tucked the wire into the collar of his shirt.

Carrie did the same with her earphones.

Fletch could hear nothing. Kriegel's mouth was moving, head bobbing, his arms waving; from the audience arms shot up, mouths stretched as wide as those of chicks hoping for food: Fletch heard nothing.

Carrie nudged Fletch and pointed.

Three little girls, standing near the women, were vomiting.

As Fletch watched, one of the women, apparently surprising herself, suddenly vomited.

Two boy children among the men were on their knees vomiting.

Several of the men in the crowd began to clutch their stomachs. They turned. They tried to run through and out of the crowd.

They vomited.

On the porch, the uniformed young man with the clipboard turned on his heel and entered the log cabin.

Kriegel's face turned ashen. His mouth was still moving but less like an orator and more like a fish.

Wolfe raised one hand halfway toward his mouth and left it there. His eyes were staring downward in alarm. He stepped to the edge of the porch.

o☉∞☉∞☉o

He vomited off the porch a wide, forceful stream.

The few men standing directly in front, somewhat below him, jumped back. Still they got splashed.

Men in the audience fell onto their knees and were vomiting wide puddles.

Others, standing over them, out of control, vomited on the heads, necks, backs of the kneeling men.

Kriegel projected vomit straight into the microphone. He fell over sideways onto the porch like a board.

Slowly, Carrie turned her face toward Fletch. Her eyes were wider than ever.

She smiled.

On his knees near them, Leary was vomiting such a steady stream he ran out of breath.

Among the crowd of men, some were puking with hands braced on their knees, others kneeling puking, others rolling on the ground clutching their stomachs as they rolled puking. The few standing, watching all this in amazement, looked like upright steel beams unaffected in a forest of trees being thrashed, laid low by a hurricane.

Apparently oblivious to all this, at the console, Jack threw a switch. Lights on the console's panel went off.

Jack took off his earphones.

Pretending to rub each ear, he removed his earplugs.

Seeing him do so, Carrie and Fletch removed their earphones and plugs as well.

Carrie gripped Fletch's arm.

Her eyes were blazing.

"What?" Fletch asked.

oᐯ∘∘ᐯ∘∘ᐯo

She nodded toward the back of Kriegel's mostly fallen audience.

There, standing, staring at them openmouthed, was their friend, the sheriff, Joe Rogers.

oOoooOoooOo

chapter 15

"No, no, no," Fletch insisted with as much conviction as he could. He and Carrie were skirting widely the ground on which the audience had stood, knelt, and puked, to get to the cabin's porch where Jack was working with his electronic equipment.

At first, Fletch had started directly across the field to speak to Sheriff Joe Rogers.

Slipping on the wet ground, the sheriff had dodged behind the trailers into the woods.

"I tell you, Carrie, the sheriff is here as a police spy, or something, taking down names, license plates. You know, doin' police business. He must be."

"Why did he run from you?"

"Because I was being stupid. He didn't want me to blow his cover."

"Sure. I'll believe that when catfish meow and climb trees."

"He's here on duty."

"He's in the wrong county for that, Mister Fletcher," Carrie said through tight lips. "He's in the wrong county, and he's in the wrong state."

Jack said to them from the porch, "That Kriegel! He sure can raise a stink, can't he?"

"Somebody sure can." Fletch and Carrie climbed the porch steps.

"How did you do that?" Clearly Carrie was willing to think better of Jack. Somehow, through electronic legerdemain, he had made almost everybody in Camp Orania vomit.

"Do what?" Jack was wrapping up his electrical wires, from microphone to speakers, console to microphone.

"Make the audience so aptly responsive," Fletch said.

Jack grinned at Fletch. "I've learned a few things. How to Incapacitate People 101."

Fletch asked, "Not 'to go with the flow'?"

"Sure." Jack laughed. "You didn't see flow?"

"There was plenty of flow," Fletch agreed.

It was almost fully dark.

Fletch looked around the camp. The sheriff had been wearing boots, jeans, and a Western shirt.

Some vehicles had left.

Bare light bulbs shone in some of the converted carports. Few of the trailers had lights on in them.

On the cabin's porch, Fletch was satisfied they were out of earshot. The men in clusters around the front of the cabin were recovering from their illness,

oⵔoooⵔoooⵔo

muttering to each other unhappily, even angrily.

"Ever hear of a Joe Rogers?" Fletch asked Jack.

"Yeah," Jack said. "You all mentioned him in the car. A friend of yours. A sheriff. Right?"

"Right."

"I looked into him for you."

"Find out anything?"

"He's an Enforcer."

Hearing Jack, Carrie widened her eyes at Fletch.

"An enforcer of what?" Fletch asked. "Who?"

"Internal security," Jack answered.

Fletch asked, "What does that mean?"

"Any of the members don't do right, he takes care of them."

"Disciplines them?"

"In a way," Jack said. "This is a secret organization. Supposed to be. As you said, 'Stupid people can't keep secrets.' "

"He kills them?" Fletch was aware his heart was beating faster than normal. "He shoots them? Are we talking about Joe Rogers?"

"Yeah. Shoots them sometimes, I guess," Jack answered. "Usually he garrotes them. With a wire. Leaves more of a message, you know what I mean?"

"Oh, God," Carrie said. "Francie!"

"Encourages loyalty among the troops," Jack said.

Fletch turned. He put his hands on the porch rail to steady himself.

Behind him, Carrie said, "Fletch . . . "

The bonfire was being lit with flaming torches by the aproned cook and another man.

The audience itself had broken up mostly into

o❍○∞○❍○∞○o

small groups of men who stood in the dark. Their camouflage shirts and pants, their boots, were well spotted with chili vomit.

Their voices were sullen. Bottles were being passed around. Even through the ever-pervasive smell from the Porta Potties, or from wherever, and the strong smell of vomit, Fletch caught the occasional sweet whiff of marijuana in the breeze. From each group of quietly talking men, one or two looked out, around at all the other groups.

Fletch guessed they were discussing their sudden, wicked illness. It had lasted well more than an hour.

He also guessed, from the way they muttered, looked around suspiciously, they were also looking for someone to blame for their illness.

If it were not the nature of these people to blame others for their ills, Fletch reasoned, they would not be here.

Anyway, what alcohol and other substances they were ingesting now were going straight into empty stomachs, onto voided systems.

One man, more than forty years old, ambled up to the edge of the porch from a nearby group. He stood on the ground, talking up to Fletch. "Did you eat that chili?" he demanded.

"No," Fletch said.

"None of it?"

"None of it."

"And you weren't sick. I didn't see you pukin'."

"Right. Eat I didn't. Sick I wasn't. Puke I didn't."

The man turned to the group he had left. "See? He didn't eat the chili. He didn't puke."

oC∞○∞o

An obscene muttering came from the group.

The man rejoined the group. "No chili. No puke," he explained.

Fletch turned.

Only Jack and Carrie were on the porch.

Shoulders hunched, Carrie was leaning on the base of her spine, her hands on the porch rail.

Jack was connecting the speaker wires to an audio disk player.

"Now what?" Fletch asked him.

"We're going to have a dance," Jack said. "You like to dance?"

"Bugaloo."

"You can bugaloo?" Jack asked Carrie. "Will you save a waltz for me?"

"Not tonight." Carrie looked around at the glistening ground. "Don't much care for your dance floor."

"Aw, shucks," Jack said. "You've got to get down."

"Not on that mess. Fletch? Don't you think we ought to get out of here, like right now?"

"What's true?" Fletch asked.

Through the dark, Fletch heard a man from another group, one near the side of the cabin porch, say, "Who's this Kriegel? Sounds like some kind of a foreigner to me."

"English," a voice answered. "He's from our English counterpart."

"German," someone said. "Kriegel."

"South African," said another.

"Sounds like some kind of foreign faggot to me," the first voice said.

The groups of men were drifting toward the bonfire.

o◯oo◯◯oo◯o

Carrie said, "I really think it's time to say good night, Fletch. I mean, get the E=MC² out of here!"

"Gee!" Fletch did not feel even slightly jolly. "Just when the dancin' is about to begin?"

"You'll want to see this, I think," Jack said. "The dance."

Recovered only somewhat, Leary was only a few meters away from Carrie.

"I don't need to," Carrie said. "I really believe I don't need to see the dance. I've seen enough."

"Give me a minute," Fletch said. "You'll stay here with Jack?"

Carrie said, "You take the worst times to pee."

Jack inserted a disk in the player. He turned the volume up. "Loud enough?"

"Can't hear you," Fletch said. "The music is too loud."

The music was martial.

Immediately, like puppets on strings, a few men around the bonfire began lifting their knees to it, marching in place, waving their bottles. In the firelight immediately their faces seemed transported into some kind of a fantasy.

Fletch ambled into the woods behind the trailers.

Once in the woods, he did not stop the sound of his own walking over dead leaves soon enough. He also did not hear over the sound of the loud, martial music.

He heard the crack against his head just above his ear. He saw the flash of light.

Knocked to the ground, he rolled over.

Sheriff Joe Rogers stood over him with a wrist-thick tree branch.

Staring down at Fletch on the ground, the sheriff said, "Shit! What are you lookin' up at me for?"

"You're in the landscape." Fletch put his hand over the lump developing over his ear. "The skyscape."

"You're not supposed to be lookin' at me!"

"Can't kill me while I'm lookin' at you, is that it, Joe?"

"Sure I can." The sheriff swung his club at Fletch's head.

Fletch grabbed the club and pulled. The sheriff began falling toward him. Fletch put one foot up and caught the sheriff in the crotch.

Then Fletch rolled out of the way of the falling sheriff.

Fletch jumped up.

For a moment, facedown, legs spread wide, the sheriff remained still on the ground.

"Are you fixin' to kill me, Joe?" Fletch kicked the sheriff's ass. "Are you fixin' to kill Carrie, too?"

Fletch kicked him again, harder. "Get up, you bastard. I want to see such a two-sided son of a bitch from the front!"

For a heavy man, the sheriff got to his feet quickly and smoothly. He stood close to Fletch.

"Son of a bitch," Fletch said. "The Enforcer for the Tribal Nation."

The sheriff said, "Chief of Internal Affairs."

Fletch scoffed. "Sure! Big titles justify anything, right? Bunch of psychotic children!"

"You could only be here for one reason, Fletcher. To destroy us. Somehow."

o{O}oo{O}oo{O}o

"You're just doin' your job, right, Sheriff?"

"You're damned right."

"Last night, you and your deputies supposedly were out in the rain looking for 'Commandant' Kriegel. You let him slip right through, didn't you? What was all that garbage you gave me this morning? Carrie was carrying one dangerous hombre on the back of her truck. I thought you were being too damned agreeable. You were pretending to be a little drunk, right?"

Eyes as wide and bright as a pickup's headlights, the sheriff took a step toward Fletch. His fists looked as big as bowling balls.

"I thought I knew you, Joe."

"You fixin' to tell me how you mean to destroy us, Fletch? Will you tell me what the hell you're doing here, or do I have to beat it out of you?"

"You can try. You've already discovered I've got a hard head."

"Talk, goddamn it, before I twist your fuckin' head off!"

The woods were flooded with the inane sound of martial music.

"I brought Kriegel here."

"Sure you did."

"You lost sight of him on my farm, didn't you?"

"The hell you brought him here. You're not one of us."

"How can you be sure, Joe?"

"I'm damned sure. I know you, Fletch. I know all about you, Irwin Maurice Fletcher."

"I guess you do, at that."

"There's only one reason you're here. You mean

○◯○○◯○○◯○

to screw up our organization somehow. I'm in an important position here. I protect these people. And you're lying. Only way to stop you from whatever you're doin' is to do you right here and now."

"And that way no one back home will ever know what a murderin', two-sided son of a bitch you are. That right, Joe?"

The sheriff smiled. "That's right, too."

Fletch said, "Don't smile when you say that."

Taking a sudden step forward, the sheriff began to wrap his forearms around Fletch's head. He tried to grab his chin, force him to the ground, possibly break his neck.

Fletch spun faster than the sheriff expected. As he spun, he raised the side of his right hand fast and hard into the base of the sheriff's nose.

Fletch thought he was free of the sheriff's reach.

Until he felt something the size of a bowling ball slam against his head.

Fletch tripped over his own legs.

Lying on the ground, he saw right in front of him the club the sheriff had used on him.

He grabbed it.

Kneeling, he saw the sheriff lunging at him.

Using both hands, Fletch plunged the sharp end of the tree branch into the base of the sheriff's stomach.

As the sheriff fell, Fletch jumped up.

Fletch clubbed the sheriff on the back of his head. On the ground, the sheriff did not move.

Fletch felt the pulse behind the sheriff's ear. It was racing. The sheriff was unconscious, not dead.

Staggering, Fletch headed back toward the main

oⴲ﹫oooⴲﹾoooⴲo

cabin of the camp. His head hurt. It felt as if all the blood in his head was congealing into an immobile mass. His neck hurt. His vision was poor.

The first time he fell to his knees he vomited. "Camp Orania," he said to himself. "Where the whole world comes to puke."

The second time he fell, he was at the side of a trailer. His legs were too weak to continue. He fought unconsciousness. He was feeling worse rather than better.

He had to clear his head. He had to get Carrie out of there.

He leaned his back against the stacked cement blocks holding up one corner of the trailer.

Even the blood in his legs seemed to be congealing. He could not move.

He just needed time, a few minutes, to clear his head, regain his vision.

In and out of consciousness, at some point he realized he had forgotten to relieve the sheriff of the small, personal gun he knew the sheriff always wore inside his boot in an ankle holster.

He also realized he had failed to search the sheriff for a wire garrote, and relieve him of that.

chapter 16

"Are you all right, Fletch?"

With the ringing in his ears, his still-blurred vision, Fletch had not heard or seen Carrie approach.

"Like a coconut," he said.

"What happened?"

"I got hit on the head."

"By what?"

"A bowling ball."

"You're not making much sense," Carrie said. "Your eyes are glassy."

"I came across Joe Rogers in the woods," Fletch said. "I thought I needed to confirm what Jack said about him. Joe was a friend."

"Looks like you confirmed the worst."

"I did."

"Poor Francie. I expect she has no idea of this at all, at all." Carrie's eyes scanned the dark woods. "Where's Joe now?"

"Taking a nap." Fletch jerked his thumb toward a place in the woods not far behind them. "I knocked him out."

"You knocked the sheriff unconscious?" Carrie's giggle sounded a little nervous.

"He'll be snoozin' a little while." Fletch fingered the lumps on his head. "How we protect ourselves from the law once we leave here I haven't the faintest idea."

"Can we leave now?"

"No." Fletch rubbed what parts of his head did not hurt too much, to encourage the blood to course. "I can't drive. I can't see very well. I can't even walk yet. Sit down. Give me a few minutes. Then we'll go."

"Poor Fletch." Still glancing nervously into the woods, Carrie sat on the ground beside him. She took his hand. "Anything I can do for you?"

"Yeah," Fletch said. "Don't sing 'Rocky Top' just now."

She said, "Not to that stupid music."

Fletch tried to focus, concentrate on what was happening in the middle of the campground.

The men generally were moving in circles around the bonfire, some clockwise, some counterclockwise. They reminded Fletch of young people in Spain, boys and girls, walking around a town plaza, a *paseo*, scrutinizing each other without looking directly at each other, while hoping themselves to be admired.

oᴄ❍oo❍oo❍o

Those who had been marching in place began to move forward around the bonfire. Some marched quickly, pretending they had marshal's batons, others shouldered rifles. As they did so, their arms flashed out at each other. In what could have been seen as friendly gestures, they slapped the backs of the heads, the shoulders of those they passed. But they were hard slaps.

Fletch winced at every slap to the head he saw.

The "dancing" was turning violent.

The men seemed to be enjoying themselves, their violence.

Most had taken off their shirts. Their sweating chests, backs gleamed in the moonlight, firelight.

At first, circling the bonfire slowly, they cuffed each other's heads, shoulders with the palms of their hands. Then, bare-chested, they began to bump into each other full-bodied, laugh, go on to bump into someone else even harder. A few got knocked down. It seemed a playful, primitive, silly game. They butted heads. A few faces became bloody. They ran up behind each other and kicked each other, hard. One older man, personally affronted, broke his bottle over a boy's head, sending him sideways onto the ground. Some paired off and began wrestling on the ground, freestyle, not according to any rules, just clutching each other, bringing each other down, rolling together over the vomit.

All this to blaring march music.

Also watching the "dancing," Carrie said, "What fun. Does this come under the heading 'Boys Will Be Boys'?"

oⒸoooⒸoooⒸo

Fletch said, "Just Saturday night at the ol' campground."

Leary was in his element. Laughing insanely, he ran around, bumped people, butted people, punched them directly in their faces.

Fletch said, "I don't know how that guy is still standing up."

Just then someone ran up behind Leary and whacked him over the back of the head with a board.

With both hands, Fletch grabbed his own head.

Leary was totally unconscious when he fell.

"He isn't," Carrie said.

Some of the younger ones were trying to do something probably they had seen in movies, which did not work for them, not karate, not kick-boxing, just some ignorant, ungainly high kick aimed at each other's throats, heads usually, which sent themselves into a facedown flop on the ground.

Watching them, focusing badly, still feeling nauseous, full consciousness coming and going, in his memory, Fletch heard Toninho say,

"Orlando . . . Give Fletch a demonstration of capoeira, *of kick-dancing. You and Tito. Make it good. Kill each other."*

This memory came from long ago and far away.

In that memory, Fletch and Toninho were sitting by an uncleaned swimming pool outside a house of ill repute in the mountains above Rio de Janeiro, Brazil.

oꙨoooꙨoooꙨo

"Wake up," Orlando said.

In a short moment, Tito and Orlando had the rhythm of it, had each other's rhythm. Gracefully, viciously, rhythmically, as if to the beating of drums, with fantastic speed they were aiming kicks at each other's heads, shoulders, stomachs, crotches, knees, each kick coming within a hair's breadth of connecting, narrowly ducking, side-stepping each other, turning and swirling, their legs straight and their legs bent, their muscles tight and their muscles loose, their fronts and their backs flashing in the sunlight, the hair on their heads seeming to have to hurry to keep up with this frantic movement. With this fast, graceful dance, they could have killed each other easily.

Eva had come onto the porch to watch. Her eyes flashed. A few faces of other women appeared in the upper windows of the plantation house. Everyone loves the Tap Dancers. . . . They're sleek.

"Remember . . . " Toninho was saying. "A skill developed by the young male slaves, in defense against their masters. They would practice at night, to drums, so if their masters came down from the big house, to look for a woman, they could pretend to be dancing. Thanks to—what is the word in English?—miscegenation, such skills ultimately were not needed. . . . "

There was a loud Thwack! and Tito began to fall sideways. He had taken a hard blow to the head from the instep of Orlando's foot. The blow could have been much, much harder.

∘⟨∘∘∘⟩∘∘∘⟨∘

Tito did not fall completely.

"I told you to wake up," Orlando said regretfully.

Recovering, Tito charged Orlando like a bull, right into his midriff. Orlando fell backward, Tito on top of him. Laughing, sweating, panting, they wrestled on the grass. At one point their bodies, their arms and legs, were in such a tight ball perhaps even they could not tell whose was whose.

Eva, moving like Time, went down to them.

Finally, Orlando was sitting on Tito and giving him pink belly, pounding Tito's belly hard repeatedly with his fists. Tito was laughing so hard his stomach muscles were fully flexed and no harm was being done.

Standing over them, behind Orlando, Eva laced her fingers across Orlando's forehead and pulled him backward, and down.

Kneeling over Tito as he was, sitting on him, bent backward now so that his own back was on the ground, or on Tito's legs, Orlando looked up Eva's thighs. His eyes rolled.

He jumped up and grabbed Eva's hand.

Together Orlando and Eva ran down the grassy slope from the swimming pool and disappeared . . .

"Ugly, isn't it?" a soft voice beside, above Fletch said.

Kriegel stood in the moon shadow of the trailer. Both Carrie and Fletch looked up at him.

Even at that distance, the light flickering from

the bonfire made the blue, saddle-shaped birthmark over Kriegel's nose seem to come and go, appear, disappear.

Fletch said, "It's not *capoeira.*"

Kriegel took a step to stand beside Fletch. "What's that?"

"Kick-boxing," Fletch said. "A skill, an art, a method of fighting developed by Brazilian slaves to defend themselves against their masters."

"Black slaves?"

"Yes. Black slaves. It is very beautiful. It is very deadly."

"Beautiful . . . ?" Kriegel watched the men staggering around the lowering bonfire aiming blows at each other with their fists, with their feet.

By now several were unconscious on the ground. Most of those still standing were bleeding from their foreheads, noses, ears, mouths.

Fletch said, "I think your education regarding this hemisphere suffers, Doctor."

Ignoring him, Kriegel said, "They are so stupid. They are all so stupid. I hope you know I realize how stupid these animals are, Mister Fletcher."

"Animals? These aren't the chosen people?"

"No. You are the chosen people, Mister Fletcher. All this I do for you."

"Don't bother."

"Never judge a leader by his followers."

"No?"

"Do not judge me by these stupid, stupid people."

"Why not?"

"We are just using these fools, these psychotics, toward an end."

oͻOͻooͻΟooͻΟo

" 'Using' them," Fletch repeated.

"Of course. Using them. I wish I didn't have to. There are many reasons you should be grateful, supportive toward my efforts."

"Sorry, I never carry my checkbook."

"Where would these psychotic fools be tonight, what would they be doing if they were not here bashing each other's brains out?"

"Home baking cookies?"

"They have to belong to something, something bigger than they are, something secret, of which they can be secretly proud. By their natures, these fools are gang members. They are incapable, you see, of standing on their own, as individuals. We're just taking advantage of their natures. We direct their energies. We organize them. They need the discipline we give them."

Fletch almost choked. "Discipline!" He rubbed his forehead with the heel of his hand. Not once had Kriegel looked directly down at Fletch, perceived Fletch's condition. "You guys have a strange idea of discipline."

"Yes," Kriegel said. "Discipline. The discipline is in the secret. As long as they belong to us, they will restrain themselves in the world, keep the secret of their group power to themselves, only do in the world what we order, only commit the mayhem we demand. The discipline is in the belief we give them of our ultimate mission. They must save themselves for that, you see."

Fletch stared through the firelight at the soft lines of Kriegel's chest, narrow shoulders, chins.

Kriegel said, "I have nothing but contempt for these fools."

o◯oo◯oo◯o

He slouched away into the dark.

After Kriegel left, Carrie said, "I'm proud of you."

"Why?"

"You didn't let the ol' fool know you're incapacitated."

"Right," Fletch said. "Siegfried."

Jack came around the corner of the building. "I was looking for you both. What are you doing here?"

"Recovering," Fletch answered.

Carrie said, "He ran into your Enforcer in the woods."

"Your Chief of Internal Affairs," Fletch said. "For some reason, he doesn't believe I'm one of you. I forgot to pull the 'Siegfried' line on him." ·

"I guess they fought," Carrie said. "Fletch won."

"He doesn't look it," Jack commented. "Where's What's-his-name now?"

"I hope he's still suffering nightmares," Fletch said. "Probably of black people taking over the world and making him pick cotton while singing in Hebrew."

Carrie said to Jack, "Fletch is barely conscious himself."

"I can tell."

"I'll be all right," Fletch said. "We'll go soon."

Jack sat cross-legged on the grass with them. He did not lean his back against the cement blocks. He could see Fletch and Carrie and also the bonfire.

The outline of the hills around the encampment was clear in the moonlight.

Conversationally, Fletch said to Jack, "You know,

this encampment is as indefensible as Sarajevo."

Jack's eyes scanned the hills. "I know. Pitiful. Almost none of these guys has any military training whatsoever."

Fletch said, "That's obvious."

"About eighty-five percent of them have spent time in institutions, but they've been either prisons or mental institutions."

"That scares me, sure enough," Carrie said. "All these ignorant messes runnin' around with machine guns and pistols, knives, steel-toed boots, chains and whips."

"Like me," Jack said. "Do I scare you?"

"Sure enough," Carrie said softly.

Jack said, "That's the point. You see?"

Fletch said, "Maybe I'm beginning to. Then again, I'm half-unconscious."

In a most conversational tone, Jack said to Fletch, "You mustn't worry, you know. My mother is very indebted to you."

"For what?" Fletch asked.

"Me." Jack's smiling face in the flickering firelight was a warm delight for Fletch to see. "I'm the light of her life."

"Sure," Carrie said. "I bet you are. You and her septic tank."

Jack laughed. "I am."

Fletch said, "Maybe."

Jack said to him, "She thinks you hung the stars in the sky."

"Why?"

"You made her life. Her career."

"Hardly," Fletch said.

"That story you gave her. The biggest scoop of her life. It established her."

"I never gave your mother a story."

"The story about the murder of the big newspaper publisher, Walter March, during that journalism convention at Hendricks' Plantation. Because she had the story, she got the job at *The Boston Star*. That story won journalism prizes for her."

"Your mother was more than capable of getting her own story, anytime, anywhere, about anything. And of winning her own prizes."

"She said you gave the story to her. The whole thing. She scooped the world with it. She said she never could figure out how you put together that story, every detail, so well and so fast. Especially seeing it seemed to her you spent almost all your time at the resort in your hotel room."

Fletch recalled the suitcase full of electronic listening devices he kept under his bed at Hendricks' Plantation.

Jack chuckled. "Mother says you not only gave her a child, me, you arranged it for her so that she could afford to have the child, me. Support me well, educate me."

"Your mother always loved to tell stories about me," Fletch said. "Just because she tells a tale doesn't mean it's true."

"Jack Saunders says so, too: you got her that job at *The Boston Star*. From there her career soared."

"You know Jack Saunders?"

Jack was a newspaper editor Fletch worked with for years.

"Sure."

∘◠∘∘◠∘∘◠∘

"How?"

"Mother and he still keep in touch. I told you: I spent some time in school in Boston. It's only natural I should know him."

Fletch had in mind several simple questions to ask. He asked none of them.

Instead, he said, "Jack's retired now."

"Yes. 'Reluctantly retired and delightfully discontent,' as he describes himself. He insists the fourth estate has slipped badly since it's had to do without him."

"He's right. You ever hear him speak of his wife?"

"Oh, yes. I believe Mister Saunders has spent his best energies thinking up terrible, rude, hilarious things to say about her."

"He has."

"I know her, too," Jack said. "They had me to dinner several times. She loves him truly, deeply, wonderfully."

"Of course. And he loves her totally."

"He says you were pretty good at your job, too."

"He does?"

"Yeah."

"He never told me that."

"Sure," Jack said. "He's told me stories about you."

"Everybody tells stories about me," Fletch said.

"And none of them is true?"

"None of them," Fletch answered. "Not one."

They were silent a moment.

His head clearing, Fletch said: "I do believe this young man is trying to tell us something, Carrie."

"Feeling better?" she asked.

o⊙oo⊙ooo⊙o

"Yeah." Slowly, Fletch stood up.

He stood still a moment, while dizziness cleared his head.

When his vision cleared, he saw that Jack and Carrie were both standing as well.

"Well," Jack said, "I guess I'll leave you here."

"Come with us?" Fletch asked.

"No." The answer was immediate and crisp.

Jack turned on his heel. Hands in the back pockets of his shorts, he walked away from them, back toward cabin headquarters.

Fletch and Carrie watched him go.

Carrie asked Fletch: "What do you know now you didn't know before?"

Fletch said: "I know we've got to get the hell out of here. Right now."

oᗣooᗣooᗣo

chapter 17

Closely followed by Carrie, Fletch worked his way
behind the trailers toward where they had parked
the station wagon and truck.

Although having to go along the edge of the woods,
in and out of them, he gave the place where he had
left the sheriff as wide a berth as possible.

He had considered walking all the way around
the opposite side of the encampment, but he feared
his head, pounding at every footstep, his legs, still
wobbly, could not take such a long hike.

He did not want to collapse again.

"FLETCH!"

"Ohhhh," Fletch said in disappointment. There
was a wire around his neck. It was being pulled
taut against his throat from behind. He had thought

he was going to succeed in getting Carrie safely out of the encampment.

While trying to get his fingertips under the wire at his throat, Fletch was flung around to his left.

In a blur, he saw Carrie sitting on the ground like a rag doll on a shop's shelf. Her legs were pedaling to get herself up.

His ears flooded with a gurgling noise.

His eyes closed.

Suddenly, still moving sideways, he was falling freely.

On the ground, he sat up.

His fingers tore the wire from around his throat.

There was a dark bulk on the ground.

A slim figure stood over it.

Bending his knees, the young man crouched and put his hands out to the bulk. He turned the bulk over.

The heavyset man on the ground was totally inert.

"Jack?" Slowly Carrie was approaching the two figures, the big, heavy man on the ground, the slim, light man crouched over him.

As she reached them, she put her hand on the young man's shoulder. "Jack . . . "

Fletch got up.

He went to them.

"Dead," Carrie said. "Poor Francie."

Still crouching, his hand on Sheriff Joe Rogers, with an ashen face Jack looked up into Fletch's face.

Jack said to Fletch: "What do you know? I've killed a cop."

o◯oo◯oo◯o

*   *   *

Together, Jack, Carrie, and Fletch continued to walk toward where the station wagon and farm truck were parked in the woods. Now they did not bother to keep to the shadows.

At first, they said nothing.

They had left the sheriff's body in the woods, well away from any natural path.

After a moment, Jack said: "I only hit him once."

Fletch said, "I guess once was enough."

Carrie was making sniffling noises as she walked.

As they approached the woods, a group of men Fletch had not seen at the bonfire came toward them. They were dragging something large and heavy on the ground.

It was the bull calf.

"Hey, Lieutenant!" one of them called to Jack. "You hungry?"

Fletch went to where the men stopped to rest. Dragging the bull calf by its hind legs and tail was tiring them.

They had shot the bull calf behind one ear. Executed it.

Fletch had not heard the shot over the music.

He looked back at Carrie, who had remained some paces away.

She was looking away in the moonlight. At her sides, her fists were clenched.

One of the men said, "We're gonna have us some bar-b-que!"

In a low voice, Jack said to them, "I'll be right back."

He and Fletch continued.

o◯ooo◯oo◯o

Angrily, Carrie had walked into the woods ahead of them.

She screamed.

When Fletch got to her, she was slapping at a man's legs dangling in the air. She had walked into them. The legs were swinging against her head and shoulders.

Fletch pulled her away from the dangling legs of the corpse.

He looked up.

He recognized the filthy apron.

"My God," Jack said behind them. "They hung the cook!"

oOooOooOo

chapter 18

"Have you filled up your condom yet, son?"

The palms of his hands were on Jack's bare shoulders. They slid to his neck and rubbed it, caressed it, gently, slowly, firmly.

"Not yet, sir."

Nearing midnight, Jack, shirtless, sat at the computer console in the small office in one of the two front rooms in the log cabin headquarters of Camp Orania. When he heard someone coming, Jack had slid Tracy's computer code book into a desk drawer, quit the modem, neatly stacked his disks and quickly typed on the blank screen, *Now is the time for all good men to come to the aid of their Tribe.*

The members of The Tribe had not waited long enough for the calf bull to be cooked over what remained of the bonfire. Having had their systems thoroughly voided, they were too hungry. After parts of the calf bull were seared only, in drunken he-man competition, mostly the members of The Tribe ate the bull in bleeding handfuls, raw.

The cabin had four rooms, two in front, one, the smaller used as the office in which Jack worked, the other, with a fieldstone fireplace, as a living/dining room, kitchen. Kriegel slept in one small room at the back of the cabin. Jack had thought Wolfe was asleep in the other. In the half loft over the back of the house, Tracy slept.

Despite the occasional yell, Jack thought nearly everyone else in the encampment was asleep, passed out, knocked unconscious, dead.

Using floppy disks he had bought at the mall, first Jack had copied every file from that computer: membership lists, names, addresses, ages, occupations, brief biographies, as well as the names and addresses of the subscribers to the monthly magazine *The Tribe,* names and addresses of contributors, locations, numbers and balances of bank accounts belonging to The Tribe under names various, and usually suggesting a charitable or religious nature.

One account in a Birmingham bank was in the name of Carston Wolfe. It had a balance of $53,285.12.

Again using Tracy's code book, and using the modem, Jack then found himself in a huge computer network. He scanned the "billboard," the messages headed "Attention All H.Q.'s," for the previous forty-eight hours.

The big news was that The Reverend Doctor Commandant Kris Kriegel had escaped the federal prison in Kentucky and would soon be among them. Commandant Kriegel would take his "rightful place" of leadership in the "international Tribal movement."

Kriegel was described as "a founder and organizer of The International Tribe, an important religious leader, historian, anthropologist, philosopher, professor, author, and activist, a leading international advocate of White Rights." It also repeated that he was "wanted for questioning" by the South African government and "most police agencies in Europe."

Nothing indicated that Kriegel had arrived safely at the camp in Tolliver, Alabama. There were several statements that Kriegel's "Freedom, Life and Safety must be protected at All Costs by Every Member of The Tribe, even at the Supreme Sacrifice of That Member's Own Life, for The Good of All."

In the "billboard" there were scores of messages to Kriegel, apparently from "H.Q.'s" in many parts of the country and the world, congratulating him on his escape from prison; most such messages were accompanied by personal statements from people expressing eagerness to work with him "in bringing a new energy, sense of purpose, dedication, discipline, and organization to The International Tribal Movement." One apparently humorously intended message suggested Kriegel never again delay himself, and the movement, by "ever again stopping to strangle a black whore *personally.*"

Also in the "billboard" file were rantings, many not really comprehensible, concerning historic, universal, and immediate, local injustices committed

oᴏᴄⒶooⒶoⒶo

by various nonwhite groups and individuals. The alphabet of derogatory names used for these groups and individuals in the "billboard" would make its own glossary.

Jack found the membership lists, et cetera, of groups around the country and the world all easily accessible from the little computer at Camp Orania in Tolliver, Alabama. Also, he found a list labeled "Those Targeted for Assassination." To his great surprise, he even found particulars regarding Germany's "Autonomen," the hooded, masked force that "protects" white rights demonstrators from German security forces.

Clearly, The Tribe was proud of its ability to document perfectly.

Also clearly, Jack thought, probably because the members of The Tribe believed in the righteousness of their cause and in the purity of their own hearts, their security systems were as naive as might be The Sisters of Charity's.

All this information Jack was copying onto floppy disks when he heard a man's heavy tread approach the little office.

When Commandant Wolfe entered the small office, Jack was typing onto the computer screen, *And Miriam and Aaron spoke against Moses because of the Ethiopian woman whom he had married: for he had married an Ethiopian woman.*—Numbers 12:1.

Caressing Jack's neck, in a low voice Wolfe asked, "You haven't filled even one condom yet?"

"No, sir."

"Why not?"

At the console, Jack sweated profusely. His floppy

oℂoooℂoooℂo

disks were plainly visible next to the computer. He hoped Wolfe was sufficiently computer ignorant not to suspect what he was doing. "Haven't had time yet, sir."

"A beautiful Aryan boy like you has no interest in sex?"

"I have interest in sex, sir."

"What are you working on?" Wolfe continued to massage Jack's neck.

"I'm typing notes for Doctor Kriegel's sermon in the morning, sir." Jack thumbed the edges of the floppy disks. "And putting into the computer some of his writings, you know, his sermons, speeches. Some of the things he wrote while in prison. Very important I get them into the computer."

"Kriegel had use of a computer in prison?"

"Of course," Jack answered. "He worked in the library. You know about the computer billboard he established among the prisons?"

"Yes."

"That was how he organized the prisoners around the country. No one could stop him. His newsletters that were mailed from Washington, Berlin, Warsaw, back to the prisoners . . . "

"Yes, yes. Our friend Kris Kriegel is a genius at organization. A spellbinder, too. What's this?" Wolfe leaned over Jack's head. From the computer screen, he read, " 'Now is the time for all good men to come to the aid of their Tribe . . .' "

With Wolfe's hands on his neck, Jack closed his eyes. He took a deep breath.

"Excellent!" Wolfe clapped him on the shoulder. "Simple, familiar statements! Exactly what is needed! Give them the familiar in a new context, and people will believe and do whatever you want! Isn't that what preachers have been doing for centuries?"

Jack sighed. "If you say so, sir."

"And what's this? 'And Miriam and Aaron spoke against Moses because of the Ethiopian woman whom he had married: for he had married an Ethiopian woman.' Moses married a nigger?"

"So it was reported, sir. Moses married interracially."

"Ah, yes. Of course." Wolfe cleared his throat. "Moses was a Jew, wasn't he?"

"Such is commonly believed."

Jack typed: *There is neither Jew nor Greek, there is neither bond nor free, there is neither male nor female: for ye are all one in Christ Jesus.*—Galatians 3:28.

"Ah, yes." Looking up, Jack saw Wolfe frown as he read. "I'm sure Brother Kriegel knows what he's doing."

"Oh, yes, sir."

Wolfe squeezed Jack's shoulders. "Still, it is so late in the night." Wolfe ran his hand up Jack's arm. "You are so sweaty. Such a sweaty boy. Don't you think it is time you filled at least one condom?"

"Sir?"

"Perhaps you need to be stimulated. Eh? You need to be stimulated a little?"

"Sexually stimulated?"

"Yes."

"By you? Sir?"

Abruptly, Jack stood up.

o🔾oo🔾ooo🔾o

In the desk's lamplight, he faced Wolfe from a meter away.

Wolfe was shirtless, but otherwise dressed. He wore his uniform-like trousers. His boots. His holstered six-shooter.

Jack said, "Sir! The regulations of The Tribe prohibit the use of liquor and or other drugs!"

Mildly, Wolfe said, "Certainly."

With a straight arm, Jack pointed through the cabin's windows. "Sir! There was wide and general use of liquor and other drugs in this camp tonight!"

"Of course," Wolfe said. "So? The boys have to blow off a little steam. More to the point."—he smiled at Jack—"we must attract them. How can we be responsible for the habits they bring with them? Someday, we will have tighter control. . . . "

"Sir!" Jack could feel his torso pouring with sweat. He guessed the dose of salt he had had at breakfast that morning had held the sweat in his body until this unfortunate moment. "The regulations of The Tribe abhor any homosexual activity!"

"Homosexual?" Wolfe's scalp, his hairline, appeared to move backward on his head. His right hand raised slightly toward the grip of his revolver.

"Anything that smacks of homosexuality. Sir!"

"Goddamn you! You think that I just suggested"—Wolfe breathed hard—"a homosexual . . . "

"You suggested stimulating me sexually. Sir!"

"That is not homosexual! You have been in prison! With nothing but men . . . " Staring at Jack, Wolfe lifted his revolver from his holster. "Are you accusing me of homosexuality? I will shoot you for saying

∘⟨∞∘∘⟨∞∘∘⟩∘

such a thing! You think I will have you saying such a thing about me? I will say I came into the office and found you stealing files from the computer!"

Jack looked at the disks he had already filled on the desk. *That would be true.*

Wolfe raised the revolver. He aimed it at Jack. "You fought with me. I had to shoot you."

In a bored, indifferent voice, Jack said, "Shoot me."

He waved a dismissive hand at Wolfe.

Jack sat on the edge of the cot along the inside wall of the office. He picked up the guitar. He picked a few notes, strummed a few chords.

Still aiming his revolver at Jack's head, Wolfe said incredulously, "You son of a bitch, you think you can charm me, or something?"

Jack nodded to him. "Yes."

Jack played and sang for Commandant Wolfe the Kander-Ebb song "Tomorrow the World Belongs to Me," from the musical *Cabaret.*

Listening, Commandant Wolfe slowly lowered the revolver. In the lamplight, his eyes glistened.

"Goddamn you!" Wolfe said.

Before he left the office, Wolfe said to Jack, "If you mention one word of this to anyone, ever, I will shoot you! I will kneecap you! I will shoot your balls off!"

Jack played the commandant to bed.

Then he returned to pulling files from the computer.

"Hi." Just before dawn, Tracy stuck his head around the jamb of the office door.

oⒺoooⒸoooⒺo

"Mornin'," Jack said.

He had copied everything from the computer and every system attached to it he could find via Tracy's code book. Labeled in his smallest hand-writing, in his own code, he had put the floppy disks back into their boxes, back into their plastic bags, doing his best to make them look new and unused.

He had been looking forward to a few moments' sleep.

"What are you doin'?" Tracy asked.

Jack said, "Wonderin' about coffee."

"You just get up?" Tracy looked at the cot at the side of the office.

"I'm up."

"I'll get coffee. Black?"

"Sugar."

While Jack stirred around the office, making the cot look more slept in, reinserting the charged bat-tery in the camcorder, he wondered if Tracy was documenting on his ever-in-hand clipboard that at that moment in history he was taking two teaspoons of instant coffee, one teaspoon of sugar, and two pints of water from the cabin's kitchen.

Jack was grateful for Tracy's sense of order.

He admired the way Tracy had established the camp's computer. So very orderly. So very compre-hensible. So very penetrable.

Everything in it had been wonderfully easy to steal.

"Here." Dressed only in underpants, Tracy handed Jack his coffee. "One sugar."

Then Tracy sat on the cot, knees drawn up, back

o◯ooo◯ooo◯o

against the wall. He was a slim teenager with dark hair, dark eyes.

"Tracy what?" Jack asked. "What's your last name?"

"Wolfe."

"Son of Carston Wolfe?"

"Yes."

Although he was tired of it, Jack swiveled the desk chair around to face Tracy and sat in it. "Is Wolfe your real family name?"

"Of course not. My father had it legally changed. For obvious reasons."

"What was your name originally?"

"None of your business, Faoni."

Jack sipped from his mug. "Thanks for the coffee."

"You've been in prison."

"Yes," Jack said.

"How are things going?"

"You mean, for the movement? Very well. In the last five years, Kriegel has organized chapters of The Tribe in every federal and major state prison in the country. Almost half the white men—at least those who have any hope of ever getting out—belong. Of course, many of them belong just to be safe while they're in prison."

Tracy stuck out his chin. "Who started it?"

"Who started what?"

"Didn't the blacks in the prisons start organizing along racial lines first?"

"Yeah," Jack said. "For protection."

"Protection against what? Aren't the majority of prisoners in this country black?"

o◯ooo◯oo◯o

"No," Jack said.

"It seems like it."

"It's a deep question. Anyway, Kriegel has developed a considerable force."

"Yeah." Bright-eyed, Tracy smiled in appreciation. "It won't be long."

"There are plans?"

"There sure are."

"Like what?"

"Not for me to say. Kriegel has been briefed. By my father. There'll be a formal meeting later today. I don't know whether you'll be allowed to attend."

"Of course I will."

"Not up to me. You think Kriegel committed that crime, got himself sent to prison on purpose, Jack? You know, to organize the prisoners?"

"God," said Jack.

"It could be. He's awesome."

"I'll say."

"My father has developed an awesome training program here."

"You enjoy it?"

"Yeah. I've become Expert at rifle and semiautomatic weapons. I qualify as Sniper. I've done hand grenades. I'm learning mortars now. We drill pretty hard, most days."

"What fun."

"Sabotage is what really interests me. Our Sabotage Corps is really growing. My father says that's where our real strength is, in sabotage."

"What did your father do before he became Commandant Wolfe?"

"Sold insurance."

"Ever in the military?"

"Army Supply Corps."

"I see."

"He's really a great salesman. He could sell snowballs to Eskimos. You heard his speech last night?"

"Yeah. Where's your mother?"

"She left us. Couldn't stand the discipline. I mean, my father needs things exactly right, he's so important and all, has so much responsibility, organizing all this. She couldn't understand that some beatings are necessary, so people won't make the same mistake twice, you know what I mean? I mean, all this is a big responsibility. My father is a great man."

"Where are you from, originally?"

"Illinois. The Land of Lincoln. I hate that. Freed the mud people."

"You were brought up this way from birth?"

"What way?"

"Oh, believing in . . . "

"White rights? Sure. My father's grandfather was stabbed by a nigger."

"Your great-grandfather was stabbed by a black person?"

"Why do you say it that way?"

"If he was stabbed by a white person, would you and your father be against white people?"

"I don't much like the way you're talkin'. Somethin' seems wrong to me about the way you're talkin'."

"Do you ever get away from here?"

"The camp? Sure. I went to The Wave Pool in Decatur once."

"Have fun?"

"Not really."

oᴼ⊂◯oo◯ooᴼ⊃o

"Why not?"

"My father wouldn't let me wear my uniform. There were niggers there. I mean, in the water. With the white folks. There were niggers everywhere I looked. I suspect some of them had knives."

"Pretty scary, uh?"

"I wasn't too scared. Just uncomfortable. They hate us."

"Who does?"

"The niggers. They have to!"

"Why?"

"Hey, Jack! Why are you talkin' this way? You're Kriegel's lieutenant, his aide."

"So?"

"Some of the words you use sound to me goddamned liberal!"

Jack smiled. "I'm just questioning your motives, Tracy. What's with this personal motivation? Sounds emotional, to me. Are you emotional? That's soft!"

"Cut it out!" Tracy put his feet on the floor.

Jack said, "It just seems to me you can't be a pure believer, Tracy, if you have a personal, emotional motivation. Haven't you read Kriegel's pamphlets? He says people with personal emotions can't be trusted that much. Gee, I don't know about you."

Tracy went to the door. Looking around at Jack, his facial expression was similar to his father's standing at the same door a few hours earlier.

Tracy said, "My father is a great man. And he says I'm following in his footsteps. I'm doing everything he asks! What we're doing is important! It's necessary! Don't you doubt me, Faoni! When the shootin' starts, we'll see just how you act! I'll

oCOooGoooOo

bet you turn into gooseflesh!"

"I don't know, Tracy." Still in his little desk chair, Jack shook his head. "I think you'd better rethink where you are, what you're doin'. To me, you sound like a real soft guy."

Tracy slammed the door behind him.

Jack chuckled. Through the office window the dawn was gray. He turned off the desk light.

"Another day." Jack yawned. "More confusion sown."

o❍oo❍ooo❍o

chapter 19

"Blythe Spirit. Good morning."

"Good morning. This is Jack Faoni. May I speak with my mother, please, Ms. Crystal Faoni?"

"Ms. Faoni is in concentration. Do you know the appropriate code, Mister Faoni?"

"Health," Jack said. *Health* had been the appropriate code in all the years his mother had been visiting Blythe Spirit, twice a year. It had never changed.

From this observation, Jack assumed Blythe Spirit did not have the high rate of recidivism as did his mother.

"One moment, please."

Jack had returned to the little office in the log cabin headquarters of Camp Orania. Since shortly after dawn he had patrolled the camp with the camcorder videotaping everything, from the main road in, the long, winding timber road, the odd, supposedly concealed pillboxes along it either side, the trailers, carport-bunkhouses, Porta Potties, the central log cabin, the flagpole, the flag, the hills surrounding the camp, the target ranges, the ancient, locked Quonset hut he assumed was for weapons and ammunition storage.

And he had videotaped the cook hanging by his neck from the branch of a tree.

Upon his return to the log cabin headquarters Jack had interrupted the breakfasts of Commandants Kriegel and Wolfe and Lieutenant Tracy by telling them of the hanging cook. Tracy had made their breakfasts.

Kriegel slapped the breakfast table and laughed. "So! It wasn't my speech that made everybody sick! For a moment there, I thought perhaps I had lost my touch! The boys knew it was the chili! So they hung the cook!"

"Damn," Wolfe said. "It's damned hard to keep a decent cook. That one wasn't bad. He could make great pots of food out of anything we gave him!"

"Better they hang the cook than the speaker!" Kriegel laughed. "That's what I say! The boys know Man does not live by bread alone!"

"Sorry to interrupt your breakfasts," Jack said. "There's another dead guy out there, too. In the woods behind the women's trailers."

"Have some eggs, Jack," Kriegel said. "You're looking tired. Didn't you sleep well? I slept wonderfully! Nothing like a good purge for the system! You young

o❍⊙∞❍∞❍⊙o

are supposed to recuperate from a difficult time faster than we older people. Let me pour you some coffee."

The four men finished their breakfasts. Wolfe and his son discussed where on the place they would bury the cook and whoever the other corpse was. Tracy was assigned to draft someone else as cook and put him to work preparing breakfast for the men as quickly as possible. Wolfe would organize the burial.

Kriegel said, "We'll postpone the church service, our Bible reading and my sermon one hour, until after you dispose of the corpus delicatessen." He laughed. "Will eleven o'clock be all right?"

"Eleven o'clock will be fine." Wolfe put down his coffee mug. "I want the men awake when they hear that that damned Jew Moses married a nigger!"

Wolfe and his son left the cabin.

Kriegel said to Jack, "Moses married a nigger? Where do you suppose that man gets crazy ideas like that?"

Jack said: "Damned if I know."

In compliance with camp security, Jack had understood, the only telephone at the camp was the one in headquarters' little office. He knew his conversation was not being overheard. Kriegel had followed Wolfe out of the cabin "to see how blue the hanging corpse" was.

The phone rang ten times before Crystal answered it. Jack was used to that. His mother had difficulty moving, even across a health spa's bedroom.

"Hey, Maw!"

"Jack, are you all right?"

oᏅooᏅooᏅo

"Fine and dandy. Except that I am in bad need of a few hours' sleep and a shower. How are you doin'?"

"As usual. I have lost a few pounds." To Crystal a few pounds was like a bucket of sand to the Sahara. "But are you all right? Tell me about yourself. Did you connect with your father?"

"Yeah."

"What do you think of him?"

"Senile."

"Senile?" Crystal asked. "Fletch senile?"

"Yeah," Jack answered. "He can't remember any of the stories you tell about him. . . . "

oᴏ◯ᴏ●●●ᴏ◯ᴏᴏ

chapter 20

"Mister Fletcher? We got us a dead man on the place," Emory announced.

"Oh, yes?"

"Yes, sir. Dead and bloatin' up real bad."

Sunday morning, head still hurting, throat sore, neck stiff, Fletch had checked the fax machine in his study and, finding nothing yet on it from Andy Cyst, took his cup of coffee out onto the upper balcony. He loved to watch the rising sun dissipate the fog that was in the farm valley most mornings.

It had been nearly midnight when he and Carrie had left Camp Orania in Tolliver, Alabama, for home.

Before Fletch left the encampment, Jack had placed his hands on the windowsill of the station wagon as if he still had something, one more thing to say to Fletch. Fletch waited, but Jack said nothing.

Fletch realized that Jack was still in shock from having killed someone, their having found the cook hanging by his neck from a tree branch.

So was Carrie, of course, and she was heading down the long dark timber road alone in the farm truck.

So Fletch said to Jack through the car window, "We've given each other interesting times so far, haven't we?"

Jack said, "I've had more boring weekends."

"The weekend isn't over yet."

Jack looked to his side. "Why are you leaving? It may be over anytime now."

Coolly, Fletch said: "I have other things to do."

Jack did not inquire.

Fletch said, "I'm a great one for confirming things."

"Isn't that how you almost just got killed?"

"One source for any story is never enough," Fletch said. "By the way, thanks for riding shotgun for us back in the woods. You had both of us fooled."

"I guess I still can't say to you, 'Trust me.'"

"Sure. You can say it," Fletch said. "I'll store the request." Then Fletch said: "Repeat after me."

"Okay."

"All bullies are cowards."

"All bullies are cowards."

"Paranoids' worst enemies are themselves."

"Paranoids' worst enemies are themselves."

"Bye."

oᴼ₀₀᎒○₀₀᎒○

"Bye."

Following Carrie on the long drive home to the farm, Fletch telephoned airlines.

Then he telephoned Andy Cyst at his home.

"Andy! I'll bet you've heard enough from me today."

"No, sir." Andy yawned. It was midnight and Andy most likely had been in bed asleep. "It's okay."

"Thing is, I'd like to set up that story regarding people with life-threatening food addictions. Specifically, I'd like to do a short feature at that place called Blythe Spirit in Forward, Wisconsin."

"You have a sore throat, Mister Fletcher?"

"A bit of a one."

"Sorry. When do you want to do the story?"

"Tomorrow."

"You mean, today? Sunday?"

"Is it Sunday yet?"

"As far as I'm concerned it is. After I go to bed and wake up, it's the next day, however early. I was brought up that way."

"Yes. Today. Sunday."

"What's the hurry, Mister Fletcher? It's a pretty soft feature."

"That it is."

"I've got it. Sorry. This is your way of getting to that Faoni woman."

"Yes."

"And you need to get to her because of some other story you're working on."

"You're thinking pretty well, for someone half asleep."

"And let me guess: the other story has something to do with those escapees from the federal prison in Kentucky. Am I right?"

"I make no promises. I'm not sure what the story is. I'm not even sure there is a story. And if there is a story, at this moment I haven't the slightest idea how I can get ahold of it, or how I can report it."

"I understand."

"Andy? To be honest, there is also a personal element to what I'm doing."

"Aha! Just as I guessed: the shapely Faoni is an old flame!"

"Therefore I expect to pay my own expenses on this one."

"We wage-slaves will appreciate that, Mister Fletcher."

"Who is free on-camera in Chicago right now? Could Cindy and Mac meet me at O'Hare Airport shortly after noon?"

"I'll check."

"I'll do the writing, of course, if . . . "

"Yes, sir, Mister Fletcher. I'll get Research to fax you everything they have about food-addicted people at the farm before dawn."

"Atta boy. Also everything about Blythe Spirit. Who owns it, who runs it, does medical insurance pay for their services, or is it a place one checks into with a credit card?"

"Yes, sir. But, Mister Fletcher . . . "

"Yes, Andy?"

"When I called Blythe Spirit they were highly protective of their patients, or clients, or whatever. What makes you think they'll be glad to see you

o○Ooo○Ooo○o

arrive with Cindy Watts and Mac and his camera on a Sunday afternoon?"

"You'll have to talk with them, of course. That charm of yours. Assure them we absolutely shall respect the privacy of their clients, except any who volunteer to be interviewed on camera, either disguised or not. Their choice."

"You don't think they might suspect an ulterior motive if I call them at midnight and say a GCN crew is arriving at teatime?"

"I believe Blythe Spirit is a private, for-profit enterprise, Andy. You know they'll be dazzled by the publicity possibilities. For them it means more clients, income, a chance to explain their meditation techniques. And you know the one thing people never can remain silent about is silence."

Andy remained silent.

Fletch chuckled. "So call Blythe Spirit early in the morning and tell them we just happen to have a crew in their area, this is their big chance—"

"Okay."

"Sorry to ask for all this at this late hour Saturday night, Andy."

"Sunday morning."

"Sunday morning."

"It's okay, Mister Fletcher. It's always interesting to see how you work. I'll bet you have a very big story here."

"Don't bet anything you can't afford to lose, Andy. Don't bet your job on it."

When he arrived home, the Jeep was in the carport as clean as new.

o⊂◯oo◯oo◯o

Thus Fletch assumed a certain matter had been taken care of.

He assumed the remains of Juan Moreno had been carted off.

The garbage bag filled with the filthy prison clothes and boots was undisturbed by the back door.

The phones were working.

Before he had poured his coffee Sunday morning, Fletch had heard Emory's truck arrive. Normally, Emory did not work on the farm Sundays.

Emory stood on the front lawn, squinting in the early morning light, talking to Fletch on the upper balcony.

"I didn't know you and Carrie made it home last night. So I came by to feed the horses and the chickens."

"Nice of you, Emory. We got home pretty late."

"I didn't know you were here until I saw the truck and the station wagon."

"We were at a dance. In Alabama."

"Was it a high ol' time?"

"I guess. You should have been with us."

"Did you do any buck dancin', Mister Fletch?"

"Not last night."

"Many pretty girls?"

"Pretty girls . . . " Fletch thought of the bare-chested men circling the bonfire knocking each other silly. "I only had eyes for Carrie, Emory. You know that."

"None you'd bring home to Mama, uh?"

"A few I might bring home to the Judge."

"That ugly, uh?"

oC**o**oo**O**oo**O**o

"Criminal."

"Mister Fletch, I thought maybe we'd lost a cow. Somethin' smelled dead. I followed my nose. To the gully. A human. A dead man in the gully. Suspect it might be one of those escaped villains?"

"Might be. All your relatives accounted for this morning, Emory?"

Emory laughed. "I never have been able to count 'em all. The mess in the gully isn't anybody I recognize, anyway."

"That's good." On the balcony, Fletch blinked in the sunlight. "Guess I'd better come look, Emory, before I call the sheriff's department."

The sheriff's department without a sheriff, he said to himself.

Fletch realized there really was not much need for him to go look. The mess in the gully was Juan Moreno, late of the federal penitentiary in Tomaston, Kentucky. Fletch had already seen him dead. He did not want to see him again.

His training as a reporter made him go down through the house, leave his coffee cup in the kitchen, walk with Emory up the fields to the gully, and peer down at what once had been relatively human.

He could not report anything of which he was not immediately sure.

"Guess I'm going to Chicago."

When Carrie came into the study in her bathrobe she was holding a cup of coffee to her lips as she walked.

At the desk, Fletch was reading through a sheaf of faxes which had arrived from GCN and Andy

∘◠∘∘∘◠∘∘◠∘

Cyst. There were several pages describing the clinical disorder of life-threatening obesity. There were two pages regarding Blythe Spirit, its founding, corporate structure, ownership, size, services offered, qualifications of senior staff, professional operating theory, licenses, etc.

There was a one-page note from Andy saying that Mac was in hospital with a slipped disk but Cindy and Roger would meet him at Chicago's O'Hare Airport shortly after noon; the administration and staff of Blythe Spirit would be delighted to see the crew from GCN whenever they arrived that afternoon, and would do their best to prevail upon "one or two patients to volunteer for interviews."

"When?" Carrie drew her legs onto the couch under her.

"Leaving as soon as I get dressed."

"You're going to see Crystal. I thought she was out of pocket."

"I hope to see Crystal."

"Maybe she'll show you her son's postcards from Greece."

"Maybe."

"What if she does?"

"I don't know."

Carrie quoted Fletch: " 'We're all mysteries awaiting solution.' "

Fletch said, "We're all histories awaiting execution."

"I don't know what else you can do," Carrie said. "I mean, you've got to try to see Crystal, soon as you can. Whatever else that kid is, or isn't, he saved our lives last night as sure as God made bedbugs.

o◖◗oo◖◗oo◖◗o

I was awake much of the night. I must have turned fourteen miles."

"I know."

"Fletch, I'm not sure what I heard, saw yesterday. All those wild-lookin' men together. Their crazy eyes. Their guns. The foul condition of the women and children. Those three guys ol' Leary kindly run off after smashin' two of their heads together. What I heard of that obscene speech. 'Mud people.' 'Children of Satan.' 'Z.O.G.' Chants of 'White rights' have been ringin' in my ears all night. Everybody throwin' up. Did Jack really cause that with his electronic gimmicks? That violent dancin' around the bonfire. Those stupid men bumpin' into each other like battery-operated toys, whackin' each other over their heads. Seein' Sheriff Joe Rogers killed with a single stroke of that boy's hand. The cook hangin' from the tree branch, his face all pooched out."

Carrie's face did look as if it had spent the night in a pail of warm water.

"Pretty rough on you."

"You, too."

Fletch said, "I'm still not sufficiently sure of anything. Maybe it's the bangs on the head I got. I still don't know why all this has happened, or what, if anything, to do about it."

She said, "I won't really know what I saw and heard until I know if Jack is really your son. Does that make sense?"

Fletch hesitated.

"I mean," she said, "if Jack is your son, what is he doing with these people? Whoever he is, why did he lead us into this putrid mess?"

"Isn't that what kids do? I've heard something like that, from parents." Fletch picked up the phone. "I've got to call the sheriff's department."

"I wish I could call Francie," Carrie said. "Guess I'll have to wait."

"Maybe forever," Fletch said.

"Aetna? How come you're workin' Sunday morning? The choir can't do without you."

"Hydy, Mister Fletcher. Everybody else seems just plumb wore out, after all this excitement about those escaped convicts, and all. Haven't heard gurgle or burp from the sheriff since sometime yesterday. He could be dead, for all I know."

Fletch neither confirmed nor denied.

"Say, Aetna, we have a dead body out here in the gully."

Carrie's eyes popped.

"You don't say."

"I do. He's been there all day yesterday, from the looks of him. His body is all swollen up. He's popped his shirt buttons and split the zipper on his jeans."

Across the room, Carrie wrinkled her face and said, "Oouu . . . "

"Do you suppose it's anyone we know, Fletch?"

"It's a good bet it's one of those escaped convicts you all have been lookin' high and low for."

"The sheriff will be glad to hear that. The boys are sort of disappointed they didn't catch a single one. I'll call him before he gets dressed. He might want to run out and take a look before church."

"You do that."

oⓞooⓞooⓞo

"Is Carrie within hailin' distance?"

"She's right here."

"Let me speak to her, will you? I got that recipe for firecracker cake from Angie Kelly I know Carrie wants real bad . . . "

Handing over the mouthpiece, Fletch said to Carrie, "Aetna wants to talk to you. Firecracker cake."

"Oh, good!" Carrie crossed the study and took the phone receiver. "Ha, Aetna, how're you this mornin'?"

Going upstairs to dress to go to Chicago, Fletch muttered, "God! We'll never get rid of that damned body!"

oⒺoooⒸoooⒺo

chapter 21

"Miami." With a flourish, The Reverend Doctor Commandant Kris Kriegel unfolded a road map of the city of Miami, Florida, United States of America, on the square wooden table in the front room of the log cabin headquarters of the newly named Camp Orania in Tolliver, Alabama. The map covered the table.

Commandant Wolfe looked down at the map. "Miami?"

"Miami!" Jack said. "Phew!"

As Tracy looked down at the map, his face glowed.

Shortly after three o'clock Sunday afternoon, only the four stood around the cabin's table.

They were meeting later than planned.

Jack had awoken in time to set up the sound

system for The Reverend Kriegel's religious service, prayer meeting, sermon, harangue, newly scheduled for eleven o'clock.

As Jack put together the sound system, he saw the burial brigade, seven men with long-handled shovels, return from the woods. They stood around him drinking water from the cabin's garden hose. He understood from the thirsty men they had dug one very big hole. They had dropped the hanged cook and the unexamined corpse of Joseph Rogers into the same hole with the shot and shredded remains of the bull calf.

The Reverend Kriegel then had said a few words over the grave. To the men's amusement, he commented on the appropriateness of "burying the cook cheek to jowl with roasted beef."

Before Kriegel's eleven o'clock service, Jack again played martial music over the sound system, as Kriegel had ordered. After their party the night before, the members of The Tribe were bleary-eyed and listless as they gathered for the sermon.

Each holding a Bible, Commandants Wolfe and Kriegel sat on camp chairs on the porch.

Looking angelic, his eyes raised to the flag, Tracy introduced "our führer, The Reverend Doctor Commandant Kris Kriegel, whom lately God has released from the talons of the Zionist government."

The congregation sitting on the ground muttered, "Heil." A few raised their right hands to chest level.

"That government," Kriegel began without preamble, "which has committed treason against every true white citizen of these great United States."

oᴄᴏᴏᴏᴏᴏᴄᴏᴏᴏo

"White rights," the congregation rumbled.

"Today," Kriegel announced, "we are witnessing the beginnings of a great, new, worldwide revolution. Some might call it the reemergence of nationalism. It is the revolution of The Tribes! We all shall rise and do glorious battle against each other! I tell you, my brothers, we must be ready to rise as a white nation! As every tribe, as every nation in this world is now doing, so must we purify ourselves, cleanse ourselves ethnically, rid ourselves of everyone who is not one of us!"

At the electronic console, Jack inserted earplugs before putting on his earphones.

Then he fiddled with some of the dials.

To his regret, it was a very pregnant woman who began vomiting first, then two children.

Very shortly, though, the men, all revelers the night before, were on their knees, puking on the ground. They tried to beat each other, their own women and children away from them with their arms as they crawled forward on their knees, to give themselves room to vomit and breathe.

On the porch, Tracy had disappeared again.

Commandant Wolfe had his hand on the screen door to the cabin when he doubled over and puked through the screen onto both sides of the door. His vomit dribbled down the door to the threshold.

Preacher Kriegel vomited sideways onto the porch's floor.

Holding their heads and their stomachs, people stood when they could and staggered away. They headed toward their trailers, their campers, their carport bunks.

o◯ooo◯ooo◯o

Several rolled onto the ground as soon as they reached shade.

So:

Lunch was not desired, prepared, or served;

Camp Orania fell into a retching silence;

The meeting between Commandants Wolfe and Kriegel did not commence until after three o'clock.

"Do you trust him?" Wolfe glared at Jack as he entered the room for the meeting.

"Oh, yes," Kriegel said.

Wolfe growled, "I don't think I do."

Jack smiled at him. "Sure you do."

"Jack is an answer to a prayer," Kriegel said. "He hasn't been with me long, but it was Jack who organized my escape from prison."

"Ummm," Wolfe said. "My son is one thing . . . "

"And I'm another, right?" Jack asked.

"Jack's like a son to me," Kriegel said. "Besides, you've seen his father."

"That's one of the problems," Kriegel said. "His father has made no commitment to us, I'd say, from the things he said."

"But he has," said Kriegel. "It was Jack's father who made my escape good. It was Jack's father who hid me out, who disguised me, got me through road-blocks, who got me here safely."

"I don't like the way that Fletcher guy talks."

"It's not what a man says," Kriegel said primly, "it's what he does that counts."

"I think I'll look into all that," Wolfe said. "I have my own resources, you know."

In exasperation, Kriegel boasted, "Jack shot a cop. A woman cop."

o◯ooo◯ooo◯o

"Well, all right," Wolfe said.

It was then that Kriegel unfolded the gasoline company's road map of the city of Miami on the table.

"Gentlemen," Kriegel said. "Be seated."

They sat at the four sides of the table.

"Even though there are only the two of us here," Kriegel said, "with our lieutenants, this is a most significant meeting. It will go down in history. Therefore I have asked Jack to record it."

Jack took the small tape recorder out of his pocket and placed it on the road map of Miami. He turned it on.

He'd had every intention of recording the meeting, asked or not.

"Tracy," Wolfe said. "Take notes."

Tracy was ready with his clipboard and pen.

"Mine is a three-point plan," Kriegel said, "which plan, by way of stating our goal, I shall describe to you somewhat backward.

"Our goal is to drive the people from Miami."

"What people?" Wolfe looked down at the map as if it offered information other than the names of roads. "Why Miami?"

Kriegel asked, "Haven't you ever heard Miami referred to as 'the capital of Latin America'?"

Clearly Wolfe hadn't. "It's a mighty sprawly city."

"Nearly all the people in it are aliens," Kriegel asserted.

"Aliens?" Tracy looked at the map, willing to see aliens.

"How do you intend to attack Miami?" Wolfe asked.

"First, by Intelligence," Kriegel answered. "Then by Sabotage. Only then by Force."

"You mean to capture Miami?" Wolfe asked.

"Oh, yes," Kriegel answered simply.

"Capture and hold it?"

"Why not? You're thinking of the armed might of the Zionist government of the United States, aren't you?"

"I am giving it some thought, yes."

"Once we have captured Miami," Kriegel said, "the area will be flooded by white Americans eager to cast off the yoke of democracy, equality, and all that crap. We will fill up Florida like a boot. Our population will flood up the coast and west even as far as Texas, Colorado, and Nevada. Miami will be our capital."

"Nice climate," Jack commented.

Wolfe said, "You think big."

"We will do this," Kriegel promised. "And we will do this within three years."

"But how? Where do we get the manpower?"

"Your organizations in this country report to me thirty thousand registered members. And I, at this moment, command half the prison population in the United States. Have you any idea how many men that is?"

Jack said, "Lots."

"Besides, we are getting increasing numbers of followers among our student populations, our other unemployed . . . Oh, yes, we have the manpower, if we attract them, train them, and use them correctly. What we need are more and more training camps set up, using this marvelous Camp Orania you have established, Commandant Wolfe, as a model." Wolfe

∞◦◦◦◦◦◦∞

tugged his shirtfront down and squared his shoulders. "Oh, yes, Commandant Wolfe," Kriegel said, "I see you becoming an increasingly important figure in this movement."

Tracy, glaring, grimaced at Jack.

"Intelligence." Kriegel looked at the road map of Miami. "We need to know where the electrical power grids are that service Miami. How to turn the city's water off. Sabotage the sewers. Sabotage the main bridges to the city to blow them up at the appropriate moment."

"There's the sea," Wolfe said, studying the map diligently. "The ocean."

"Yes." Kriegel brushed that corner of the Atlantic Ocean with the back of his hand. "I expect the aliens to escape by sea. Back to Latin America. And New York."

"But they can ship food and water, troops into Miami by sea," Wolfe pointed out.

"There won't be time."

"Sir?" Tracy asked. "How can we attack Miami if we've already blown up the bridges ourselves?"

"That's the charm of the idea," Kriegel admitted. "Have you ever heard of a fifth column? The Trojan horse? Our troops will already be in the city. After the power and water are off thirty-six hours, first we seize the airport. And then our troops will proceed block by block, driving the aliens toward the sea."

"Phew!" Jack said. "They will drive the aliens toward the sea!"

"There won't be enough ships to take all the aliens away," Tracy said.

"Then we drive the aliens into the sea."

o‿OooⲞoooⲞo

"Drive the aliens into the sea," Jack repeated.

Wolfe asked his son, "Are you getting all this down, Tracy?"

"Oh, yes, sir."

Wolfe sat back. "Seems simple enough. Tell me, Commandant Kriegel: how do we get the money for all this, for all the training we will need to do?"

"Lots of little Miamis," Kriegel said. "We shall establish a model. Within six weeks, I should think, after you train your men for this specific task, Commandant Wolfe, we will take just the men you have here—having chosen a small, fairly isolated city, in the Southwest, South, Midwest, West, it doesn't matter—gather intelligence on it, turn off its power and water, attack it in force, and liberate from that town's banks and other businesses what I think you Americans call 'cash money.' Millions and millions of dollars of cash money."

"Ummm." Wolfe studied the matter. "Plundering. I like that idea. Will we try to hold these small cities?"

"No," Kriegel said. "Just plunder them. You'll strike without warning, lock their police and other tiny town tyrants in their own jails, and make off, overnight, with every bit of cash and other valuables you can find."

Wolfe slapped the table with the palm of his hand. "Excellent! I'm with you!"

"The rest of my plan concerns you and me, my dear Commandant Wolfe!"

"Don't you 'my dear' me," Wolfe said quietly.

"I intend to make my headquarters here, in this

encampment, to which I have given the name Camp Orania."

"You are most welcome."

"Immediately, using whatever resources you have available, I shall need a handsome house built here for myself and personal staff. Large and beautifully furnished. And air-conditioned. Complete with swimming pool."

Wolfe blanched. "Of course."

"We must have the prestige of leadership, you see."

"Certainly."

"The membership, as it swells, won't respect us without. I will need here a praetorian guard, men loyal absolutely to me and my safety. I will need similar domiciles in other parts of the country, with safe and well-planned escape routes out of and into each."

Wolfe blinked several times.

"Come now," Kriegel said. "Lieutenant Tracy has given me printouts of greetings from headquarters all over this great country and this great world. You must have my leadership. I insist things be done right. I shall have what I need."

Wolfe considered this.

Jack said, "Also the helicopters."

"Yes," Kriegel said. "Obviously I will need to be transported in and out of these encampments around the country by long-range helicopters."

"More than one?" Wolfe asked.

Kriegel said, "They have so much downtime."

"Also he'll need at least one escort helicopter," Jack said.

oᴏ⃝ₒₒₒ⃝ₒₒ⃝ₒ

Kriegel laughed. "Not to worry!" He put his hand on Wolfe's arm. "You see why it is important to put my plans into effect immediately! First thing in the morning you must begin training your men for our first plunder of a small city! To build up respect for us! To build up our membership! To build up our coffers! To give me the freedom to get around, meet with the other commandants, organize, for you to initiate training according to this plan, to work toward our goal!"

"Miami," Jack said.

Kriegel stood up. "To Miami!"

Tracy jumped up. "To Miami!"

"One last thing," Kriegel said before leaving the room. "Something must be done about the sanitation of this place. Every time I begin a speech, people throw up. It wasn't the way the cook cooked. They hung him. It certainly isn't my speaking. It must be the water."

"That's right," Jack mused. "It must be the water."

chapter 22

"Pardon me, sir. Are you Mister Fletcher?"

"I am."

The young man dressed entirely in white said, "One of our patients, Ms. Faoni, has expressed a wish to meet you. Would you mind?"

Fletch smiled. "Not at all. Where is she?"

"In her room. She's been concentrating on her weight problem, but . . . " The young man shrugged. "Will you follow me, please?"

"Sure."

Fletch followed the young man through the corridors of Blythe Spirit's second floor. Fletch now knew the place had been built as the estate of a Wisconsin timber baron.

Cindy and Roger had met Fletch at O'Hare International Airport at about one-fifteen. Together they had driven in the Global Cable News van the 112 miles from Chicago to Forward, Wisconsin.

Roger drove at first, while Cindy, who would do the on-camera work on the television feature describing Blythe Spirit's therapy for those suffering food addictions, studied the material faxed to Fletch on both the problems specific to food addiction, and Blythe Spirit itself. Fletch had studied the material on the airplane from Nashville to Chicago. Together, in the backseat of the van, they worked on the script Fletch had drafted on the airplane.

After Cindy had absorbed the material, she drove the van. She said driving relaxed her.

They were warmly greeted by the staff of Blythe Spirit.

Staying off camera, Fletch helped Roger set up the exterior shots. Once inside, he helped both Roger and Cindy set up the interview locations, helped those to be interviewed, administrators, staff, and two or three willing patients, understand what was wanted from them, helped Cindy and Roger understand what points in particular the interviewees wished to make.

When Fletch was summoned to Crystal Faoni's room, Cindy was just about to begin an interview with a patient in the sunroom on Blythe Spirit's second floor.

There was little or no need for Fletch from that point forward.

To get to Nashville Airport in time, Fletch had skipped breakfast. He had eaten an apple in the car. There was no time for him to eat anything at

oOoooOoooOo

the airport. Nothing but drinks had been offered on the airplane. He had not wanted to delay Cindy and Roger at O'Hare Airport by stopping to eat.

It was late afternoon.

Fletch was very hungry.

He did not know how to ask the staff of Blythe Spirit for food.

As they approached the door to Room 27, the young man in white slowed and spoke quietly to Fletch.

"If you can understand, sir, to ensure her privacy, Ms. Faoni has expressed the wish that she remain behind a curtain while she meets with you. You do understand, don't you?"

"A curtain?"

"Some of our patients are more sensitive about their condition than others are."

"Okay."

Fletch's stomach growled.

The room into which Fletch was shown was a perfectly pleasant bedroom. The king-sized bed and its side table were lower than usual. Two uphol-stered chairs had uncommonly wide seats. There were paintings of farm scenes on the beige walls. The outer wall was a sliding glass door onto a small balcony.

The privacy curtain hanging from a rail around the bed had been run back. It pretty well concealed the space on the other side of the bed. The curtain was a white plastic, very like a shower curtain.

Through the opaque curtain, backlit through the glass door, Fletch could see only the outline of a large bulk covered with white material. There was

o◌⊙◌◌◯◌◌◌o

a globe on top of the bulk. The globe had neatly parted dark hair.

It took Fletch a moment to realize he was seeing a seated figure, a person.

From behind the curtain, a voice said: "By my calculation, Fletch, it has taken you less than forty-eight hours, since your first meeting Jack, to find me, and to penetrate my ultimate line of defense."

The voice was that of Crystal Faoni.

"Hello, Crystal. I wish I could say it's nice to see you."

"It really wouldn't be, you know."

"How did you know I was here?"

"I heard your voice. I watched you in the court-yard through the window."

"You still didn't have to invite me in for a visit."

"I had figured you would do something to get to me. I wasn't sure whether I would see you. . . . "

"You expected me?"

"I know you."

"Yes. You do."

"You arrived with a camera crew from Global Cable News."

"Yes."

"Clever. I'm sure the owners and administrators of Blythe Spirit are delighted by the publicity."

"They've been most cooperative. So why did you decide to invite me to your room?"

"Once I saw you . . . You were counting on that, weren't you? . . . You've changed little. Are you sit-ting?"

Fletch realized he had the advantage. She was backlit by the fading light in the window behind her.

o〇ooo〇ooo〇o

The attendant had closed the door behind Fletch. He could see her amazing outline. She couldn't see him at all. "No."

"Sit down. Please."

The arms of the chair in which Fletch sat were too far away from his body to be useful. Could he have lost that much weight since that morning? "Thank you. I seem to remember a time when you and I fell through a curtain very much like that one."

"I remember, too. We were wet, and we were naked, and it was wonderful. That reporter came into the bathroom—what was her name?—and found us on the floor struggling to get out from under that damned shower curtain."

"Freddie Arbuthnot, who I thought was an impostor."

"We were laughing. I was afraid you'd use her interrupting us as an excuse to stop. You didn't."

"No. I didn't. She went away."

"You never were easily embarrassed."

"Is Jack my son?"

"What do you think?"

Various images went through Fletch's mind: the back of the lanky young man dressed in wet, muddy prison denims in his study, looking away from him, the quick flash of his eyes; an hour later finding him cleaned up in the study, as shiny as a new penny; his sitting in the morning sunlight on the top rail of the corral; his fiddling with the knobs of an electronic console in the dusk at Camp Orania; his crouching over the body of the man he had killed the night before; his repeating what Fletch said through the station wagon window just before Fletch left the encampment. "Yes."

"He is."

"People mark a certain physical resemblance."

"Mental, too. He's as curious as a cat. In spirit, he's you all over again. Do you find him witty?"

"Witty? Half."

"Do you like him?"

"Depends."

"You love him."

"Crystal, why didn't you ever tell me we have a son?"

"How angry are you about that?"

"Very."

"Why?"

"It might have been nice. You know: son and Dad; Dad and son. Birthdays. Football."

"Having a kid is a lot more than birthdays and football, Fletch."

"Did you think me entirely irresponsible?"

"How many times have you been married? Three?"

"Yes."

"Did you ever have kids with any of your wives?"

"You never really knew my wives. I mean, you did know me. We weren't grown up. I have no idea why I married Linda, Barbara."

"You believed in the old institutions, you used to say."

"Yeah."

"In a time and a place when you yourself were changing the old institutions more than you knew. We all were."

"Technology changed them more than anything

o○○○○○○○○○

we did. The bicycle. The car. Radio, television, telephone, the computer. The pill. Time and spatial relations, human relations were changing more and faster than ever before. We struggled to keep up. Most of us failed, I guess."

"You never had kids with your wives, did you? So I should snatch a kid from you, and surprise you with it? How would you have felt about that?"

"I might have liked it."

"You married some East European princess. I read you called her Annie Maggie. Did you love her?"

"Yes."

"Would you have had a child by her?"

"She was pregnant when she was assassinated. I thought only we and one doctor knew about it. It may have been the reason she was assassinated."

"Oh, God. Sorry, Fletch."

"Life is long; life is short."

"I did you a big favor, Fletch."

"How's that?"

"If you had raised a son, he would have rebelled against you, dissented, probably become the opposite of everything you are and everything you stand for. Sons do that."

"Some sons, I guess."

"Your son would have. I'm certain your son would have. Not knowing you, Jack adores you."

"Sure."

"He does. He's enormously curious about you. He has scrapbooks of newspaper clippings about you. I had to consider putting him in therapy when Princess Annie Maggie was killed, he was that upset.

o০০০০০০০

He's read your book on Pinto, Edgar Arthur Tharp, Junior, so many times, I think he's worn out a dozen copies."

"Really?"

"I think he's memorized every line of it."

Fletch recollected the faddy little argument Jack had given him about *Pinto*.

Crystal said, "He insisted on going to your college."

"He went to Northwestern?"

"Only because you went there."

"Crystal, you filled him up with silly stories about me."

"Sure. A mother who doesn't encourage respect for the father in her son loses the son. Also loses the father. Some things never change. I told him stories about how many times and in how many ways you dodged picking up that Bronze Star. He pestered me for years trying to figure out how he could pick up your Bronze Star for you, get ahold of it. He probably will figure it out yet."

Fletch asked, "Whose name is on his birth certificate?"

"Yours."

"Oh, my." Fletch wondered what would be the next thing he would eat, and when.

"That's right."

"His name is John Fletcher Faoni?"

"Yes."

"Who's John?"

"You wanted more of Irwin Maurice maybe?"

"No."

"There was no John. Don't be funny."

∘◦◯∘∘◯◯∘∘◯∘

"Your office says John Fletcher Faoni is spending the summer in Greece."

"He isn't. As you know, he is now at a camp in Alabama."

"Some camp. Crystal, there never has been a John Fletcher Faoni in any federal or state prison in the United States. We checked."

"Yes and no. No and yes. He was in the federal prison in Tomaston, Kentucky, five weeks. As a plant."

"A plant."

"As soon as he escaped from the prison, all records of his having been there were to be expunged immediately."

"He never shot a cop, or shot at a cop?"

"Of course not. Cop killing is one of the crimes that most impresses The Tribe."

Fletch snorted. "Pink Cadillac convertible. I knew the little bastard didn't know how to load a .32. Who arranged for him to enter the prison, and why?"

"I did."

"Goddamn it! You helped arrange for a handsome kid like that to spend time in a maximum-security federal prison? Have you no idea what could have happened? What probably did happen to him?"

"Nothing happened to him."

"How the hell do you know?"

"Jack is expert in a very esoteric form of the martial arts."

"Big deal! Some of those guys—"

"Besides," Crystal said, "he plays the guitar nicely."

"So goddamned what?" Fletch also wanted to shout

at Crystal, *I'm hungry!* He didn't dare.

"Lots of people helped in the arrangements, Fletch."

"Like who?"

"Jack Saunders."

"Saunders? He's retired."

"He's still meddlesome. The Attorney General of the United States. I've made a lot of friends since you last knew me."

"Friends?"

"Jack is, and always has been, determined to follow in your footsteps."

"I tried to get into prison once, do a story. No one would let me."

"This is a special case. There's a real need for what he is doing."

"Like what?"

"Jack went to Boston University's School of Journalism. He spent a lot of time with Jack Saunders and his wife. Jack, that is Jack Fletcher—"

"Jack Fletcher Faoni."

"So his name is backwards. Jack wanted to do his master's thesis on The Tribe. Secret organization though it is, he had come across it in the universities, in the streets. In fact, they tried to recruit him. Your dear old editor, Jack Saunders, suggested he treat it as a story, do it right, as something that could be published, something useful."

"Son of a bitch."

"We discussed it."

"You and Jack Saunders?"

"Jack Saunders and I."

"You didn't discuss it with me. For whom is he

supposedly doing this story?" Maybe Fletch could find a steak somewhere, on the way back to the airport, a rare steak. . . .

"Do you think it is anything that might interest Global Cable News?"

"I see. I was conned."

"Oh, I think anyone would be happy to have this story. Looks like you'll have to negotiate for it." Crystal laughed. "Then I happened to be having a conversation with the Attorney General."

"Of the United States."

"He got back to me, and asked to see Jack. The idea of using Jack appealed to him. There had been a plan to send a young FBI agent into the prison. Inmates in a maximum-security prison would spot a trained agent in a blink of an eye. After meeting with Jack, the AG was certain Jack could carry this off. Jack gets the story rights."

"Uh-huh!"

"There is this man, Kris Kriegel—"

"We've met."

"He's very intelligent, apparently."

"He's a jerk." Fletch looked around the room. There wasn't even water to drink, to fill up his stomach.

"In jail for murder."

"Yes. Was."

"Using his civil rights as a federal prisoner, he organized and took control of the white supremacist movement, established what is called The Tribe, in every federal and state prison in this country. Race riots were happening in the prisons with increasing frequency. They were becoming more vicious. Kriegel had contacts, more than that, position and authority not only in the supremacist movement outside the prisons, in this large country, but also in similar movements in Europe, Africa, and around the world. He was organizing a worldwide movement from his jail cell! They couldn't take his civil rights away from him without giving him publicity. They moved him from prison to prison, but that only made things worse, increased his contacts with the prison population, made him more powerful. They knew if they put him in solitary under some pretext, the whole prison system would explode. He was becoming impossibly dangerous. Jack was really on to something."

"So?"

"So it was arranged for Jack to go to prison to win Kriegel's confidence, arrange his escape, and to stay with him, and to find out everything he could about his contacts, the organization, the Tribe, his plans. . . ."

Fletch shook his head. "Strooth, it's a hell of a story, if I do say so myself. Hell of a master's thesis. But couldn't the kid just have written about the First Amendment like everybody else?"

"Jack's not like everybody else. He's like you."

"I didn't have a mother as willing and weird as you are! You arranged for the kid to go to prison!"

"We all did. It was what Jack wanted. He had an ulterior motive of his own, you see. Stop clucking!"

"I'm not clucking." It was getting dark outside and Fletch's mind was settling on pizza. "I'm expostulating."

"Listen to me! It was arranged that if he did not succeed immediately in attracting Kriegel, Jack would be out of there in six hours."

"Out of prison?"

"You're forgetting something. In prison, once he had Kriegel's attention and support, no one would dare touch him. Not in any way. Jack was as safe as if he were at home in bed."

"Horseshit."

"Nothing happened to him."

"You know that?"

"I do."

"So what was his 'ulterior motive'?"

"You can't figure that out?"

"Maybe. Tell me."

"To meet you. On your own turf. To do as you used to do. Still do, I guess, if I view my GCN correctly. And to do it to you."

"Do it to me."

"He didn't want to approach you as a slavering kid. He didn't want to meet you as a pedestrian while you were on horseback. He wanted to meet you while he was working on his own big story, see if he could suck you into it, see if he could make you go along with him, if he could interest you in what he was doing, in him. Apparently he did, at least to some extent. He wants your respect, too. Surely you can see that."

"You're a weird mother."

"I have one other suspicion regarding his motivations."

"What?"

"I think he was scared shitless by what he was doing. I think he wanted you with him."

Fletch remembered Jack standing by the car last

○◯○○○◯○○○◯○

night. He had something to say. He didn't say it.

Did Jack know the truth between father and son could only be bridged by the mother?

What Jack did say was, "Trust me."

And Fletch had answered something like he would store the request.

Now Fletch knew who Jack was.

And he knew something, specifically and generally, about what Jack wanted from him.

Fletch exhaled two lungfuls of breath.

"I haven't . . . " Fletch cleared his throat. "I haven't much experience . . . at responding to situations like this."

Crystal asked, "You want to know what Jack thinks of you now, Fletch?"

"No."

"He thinks you're senile." Crystal laughed. "He says you forgot all the stories I tell about you."

Fletch looked sharply at the curtain. "You couldn't know that, Crystal, unless he's talked to you, recently."

"He called this morning. From Camp Orania."

"He took a chance telephoning from there, didn't he? And how come he can get through on the phone to you and we couldn't?"

"He's my son. He knows the appropriate password. And you don't."

"You could have saved a hell of a lot of bother."

I'm hungry!

"Jack says he's doing very well. He's videotaped the camp and everyone in it. He spent the night copying all of the files out of The Tribe's computer system, files from around the country and around the world. This afternoon, he was to attend some kind of a planning meeting. That must have been interesting."

"He told you about making everybody puke while Kriegel was speaking?"

"Oh, yes." Crystal laughed. "Shades of his father.'"

Fletch did not ask if Jack had told his mother that the night before he had killed a man, to save the lives of Carrie and Fletch.

"Stop selling him to me," Fletch said. "I've got the point."

"Last night he even discovered a list of people targeted for assassination by The Tribe. Guess what."

"What?"

"Your name's on it."

Fletch thought. "I suppose it would be."

"Irwin Maurice Fletcher."

Fletch sat forward in the oversized chair. "Those sons of bitches know Jack's my kid."

"Do they?"

"He's in danger!" Fletch jumped up. "I put him in danger! Shit! End of story! To hell with Blythe Spirit! Good-bye."

Fletch left Crystal's room.

In a moment, he returned. He leaned against the doorjamb. "Crystal, what are you doing here?"

"Slimming," she said.

"Jack tells me you've been coming here twice a year for years. And you're still slimming?"

"This time they're recommending I stay here, maybe, for good."

"Are you serious?"

o◯oo◯ooo◯o

"I'm sick, Fletch. I've got a problem."

"You realize you referred to your being *incommunicado* here at Blythe Spirit as your 'ultimate line of defense'?"

"Okay. I did. So what?"

"Ultimate line of defense against what? Me? Jack? Living? Why do you need it?"

"You know all about addictions now? You got a better idea?"

"Always."

"Tell me."

"First: trust us."

"Whatever that means."

"Second: lower the food thermostat in your head."

"Oh, Fletch. What do you know?"

"I know I'll be back."

o⦿ooⵔⵔoo⦿o

chapter 23

"Time to go," Fletch said quietly. "Time to get you out of here."

"Uh?" Jack's head raised from the pillow. He looked at Fletch in the door. He sat up on the cot and swung his feet onto the floor. "I'm ready to go."

For a long moment Fletch had stood in the door of the little office in the log cabin headquarters at Camp Orania looking at his son. Jack was asleep on the cot against the wall. The room was lit only by the desk light. Dressed in shorts, T-shirt, socks, and sneakers, Jack was sprawled on the cot, his face squished on the pillow. He slept soundly. His hair was tousled. To Fletch he looked so young. Fletch wondered how his son had looked when even younger, as a boy, a child, a baby, asleep, awaking, awake, playing, listening, laughing, crying, happy, angry, bored. Standing in the door just watching his son sleep, Fletch realized something of how much he had missed.

It was dawn, Monday.

Sitting on the edge of the cot, Jack shook his head. "I was wondering how I was going to get out of here."

Fletch said, "There is a thick fog."

Fletch had had to fly from Chicago back to Nashville through Atlanta at that hour of the night. He had left his car at the Nashville airport.

He had eaten three sandwich suppers since leaving Blythe Spirit.

In the fog the drive from Nashville to Tolliver, Alabama, had been slow. Even though Route I-65 was a good, clear highway, he had not dared drive faster than the speed which would allow him to stop safely within half the distance of his visibility.

Finding the entrance to the timber road into Camp Orania proved a challenge. In the fog he went by it three times before finally spotting the sentry box a few meters down the road.

He stopped at the sentry box, prepared to say, "Code name: Siegfried." No one came out of the box to challenge him.

Once in the main area of the encampment he parked the station wagon in the woods, facing outward, toward the main road.

The only light was in the front right room of the headquarters log cabin. He crept onto the porch, through the screened door quietly, and pushed open the door to the office.

Fletch asked, "Were you waiting for me?"

Jack said, "I don't know."

"Let's get out of here."

Dawn light was penetrating the fog.

From somewhere in the camp there was the sound of one man, alone, roaring with what might have been laughter. It was a high sound, sporadic. It sounded nervous, uncertain, crazed.

Fletch said, "I guess Leary is up."

"Yeah," Jack said. "He's been mixing coke and booze and God knows what else."

"Not what he needs."

"Not what anybody needs."

Jack took a plastic shopping bag from the kneehole of the desk. In it were computer disks, audio and videotapes.

From outside, closer, Leary roared with insane laughter. It was the same laughter he had uttered just before he had smashed his forehead against another man's.

Then there came the rapid fire of not one but two semiautomatic weapons.

Fletch glanced through the window.

Leary was standing near the flagpole. He had a semiautomatic weapon in each hand. He was firing both weapons in a full circle around the camp.

He was yelling, "Get 'em! Get 'em, guys! They're everywhere. Get 'em now!"

As Fletch saw Leary pivoting to face the cabin, he ducked. "Down, Jack! Get down!"

"What's happening?"

"Leary's shooting up the camp!"

"Has he gone crazy?"

Shells came through the window glass. The desk lamp shattered.

Fletch sprawled on the floor.

There was the sound of other firing, a lot of it. Men were yelling on all sides of the camp.

Jack reached up to the desk and grabbed the camcorder. " 'Paranoids are their own worst enemies,' " he quoted.

He crawled through the door of the office to the cabin's front screen door.

"Wait a minute," Fletch said.

"No, no."

"Jack!"

Jack pushed open the base of the screen door. He continued crawling on his stomach out onto the porch.

"Jack, no!"

Fletch crawled after him. He grabbed Jack's leg.

Jack pulled his leg free of Fletch's grip.

Fletch saw that on the muscle at the top of the calf of Jack's left leg was a tattoo of a small, wide-opened blue eye. It was complete with lashes. It stared behind Jack.

Fletch had not noticed the blue-eye tattoo on his son's leg before.

He laughed.

The screen door closed behind Jack.

Fletch remained on the floor inside the screen door. He was not much safer than Jack was.

Through the door Fletch could see the figures with their weapons standing on all sides of the camp in

∘◦◦◯◦◦◯◦◦◦

the fog. They could have been anybody, friends to each other or foes.

They came out from cover while still pulling on their pants, stamping their feet into boots.

They were shooting around the hills above them.

They were shooting around the camp.

They were shooting each other.

At the base of the flagpole, Leary was dead meat.

In the fog the figures with their spewing weapons took on the postures, the poses of comic book characters, cartoons. They stood bravely, stupidly in the open, feet separated, knees a little bent, shoulders low. They fired their weapons from their waists. They sprayed bullets every which way. They shot at every noise they heard, at every figure they saw, at anything that moved.

Hit by fire, they even fell like comic book characters, some rising up and sitting down hard, then rolling on the ground to accept death. Some flung their arms up dramatically, then dropped their weapons before falling themselves.

To Fletch, these men seemed to rush to their deaths, savor it. They did little or nothing to protect themselves.

On his belly on the porch, Jack was taping it all.

In the increasing light, few now were firing toward the cabin headquarters.

"God! The stupid bastards!" Wolfe was on the floor beside Fletch, looking through the bottom of the screen. "Jesus! These goddamned fools! I hate them! Look at what they're doing to each other! How many are dead so far?"

oᴑooᴑoooᴑo

Fletch said, "About twenty."

Kriegel, his girth dressed only in a towel, stepped between Fletch and Wolfe. He pushed open the screen door.

On the porch, Kriegel raised his arms. He yelled, "Stop firing!"

"Were we attacked?" Wolfe asked Fletch.

"Yeah. By Leary."

"Leary! Why?"

"Guess he got a snootful."

Tracy was on the floor beside Commandant Wolfe. Blood had drained from the boy's face.

"Stop shooting!" Kriegel shouted. "Stop! Stop!"

Arms still raised, Kriegel stepped off the porch. Yelling as loud as he could in all directions, he began to cross the encampment toward the flagpole. "Stop! Stop, listen to me! Stop shooting, you damned swine!"

Five meters from the cabin, Kriegel was shot in his right leg. He spun around with the shot.

Holding his bleeding leg in his hand, he continued across the encampment.

Within another couple of meters he was hit in the chest and face.

That time when he spun, he fell to the ground and stayed there.

"Jesus!" Wolfe said. "These guys! These stupid, damned . . . "

The firing continued for some minutes.

The encampment was littered with bodies. A few still writhed. Except for the pain and the crying these few were as good as dead.

Then there was a long moment of silence.

o◖oo◖oo◖o

On the porch, Jack was checking his camcorder. Wolfe stood up and went through the screen door. Tracy followed Fletch onto the porch.

Hands in the back pockets of his uniform pants, Wolfe stood at the top of the steps and surveyed the carnage.

Fletch asked Jack, "Did you get it all?"

"Yeah."

"Even through the fog?"

"Oh, yeah. This has an 8 to 1 focus."

"You could see them better than they could see each other."

Jack left the porch.

He moved around the camp, videotaping every corpse.

Fletch asked Wolfe, "Do you suppose there are any we can try to save?"

Wolfe said: "Who gives a shit?"

From the direction of the trailers where the women and girl children lived, they came and stood together in a wide-eyed, unmoving, silent group. They came so far and no farther.

Jack came back toward the porch.

"How many dead?" Fletch asked him.

"Thirty-six. Two still suffering. Those two are beyond help."

"How many were in the camp?" Fletch asked Wolfe.

"Forty-one."

"I guess a few slept late."

Wolfe said, "They're under their beds. Bastards. All of 'em. There was nothing I could do with them. Such fools, useless, dumb fools."

oᴑooᴑoooᴑo

Fletch held Jack's shopping bag of disks and tapes. "Let's go," he said to his son.

Jack dashed into the log cabin. He came out carrying the guitar by its neck.

Wolfe asked, "Where? Where are you going?"

Fletch shrugged. "Out into that big, scary world out there, I guess."

At the sound of the whimpering, Fletch turned back to survey the encampment.

Like a sniffing puppy, Tracy, in his uniform, was darting from one dead body to another, looking at each for a moment, wringing his hands, making this most pitiful noise of distress, fright, shock.

On the porch, Wolfe drew his pistol from his holster. He waved it vaguely in the air.

For a moment, Fletch was unsure whether it was Wolfe's idea to shoot at Jack and Fletch, or to shoot himself.

While Fletch watched, Wolfe slumped down onto a camp chair. He lowered his head. He held his pistol between his knees.

Yellow sunlight was breaking through the fog.

Wolfe's hair turned brassy in that sunlight.

The dead bodies strewn on the ground began to cast shadows.

o◯〇oo◯oo〇o

chapter 24

There were still patches of fog in the low places but for the most part Fletch drove Jack through a dazzling sunny morning toward Huntsville Airport.

It was hard for each of them to assimilate what he had heard, seen, experienced, felt in a foggy encampment surrounded by woods just minutes before.

As Fletch turned onto the road away from the encampment, Jack had asked: "We're not reporting this?"

"That's the point, isn't it? To report it?"

"I mean now." Jack glanced at the cellular phone on the car seat next to Fletch. "To the cops or something."

"You said there was no need for medical attention. Right?"

"Yeah," Jack said. "Those who were dying are dead. Those weapons don't leave many survivors."

"You'll need time to do the story. Wolfe can report the mess. If he will. Let's not blow the story."

"I've heard that about you. You once reported a murder to your editor and asked him to tell the photographers to give the widow time to get home to report the murder."

"Did I?"

"You just said I've got a story here." Jack patted the plastic shopping bag on his lap.

"Oh, sure. And you think it's a little hotter, more immediate than a master's thesis?"

"Well, don't you?"

"I don't know. I've never read a master's thesis, let alone written one."

"For whom am I doing this story?"

"You mean, for which news organization?"

"Yeah."

"Your choice. It's your story."

"Don't you have some sort of influence at Global Cable News?"

"Me? Not much."

"You're consulting/contributing editor for GCN."

"Well, yeah. They pick up the phone to me."

Jack looked out his window. "I guess I could call Jack Saunders. He must know somebody who would be interested in this story."

"Yeah," Fletch said. "You might do that."

"But I've got all this videotape," Jack said. "What would the print press do with it?"

"Good point. Well, we might give GCN a try. If that's what you want to do." As he drove, Fletch

oϾϿoooϾϿoooϾϿo

pressed Andy Cyst's home number into his cellular phone panel. "Andy! Sorry to wake you up."

"Yes, Mister Fletcher," Andy slurred into the phone. "It's all right, Mister Fletcher. Really."

"Come on, now, Andy. I haven't bothered you since yesterday."

"Yesterday: Sunday. The day before: Saturday."

"Do you guys think you'll be able to make anything much out of that Blythe Spirit story?"

In the car, Jack's eyes cut to Fletch.

Andy's voice became more awake. "Actually, Mister Fletcher, it may turn into a good story. We're surrounding it with talking heads, other experts, to give their opinions on the therapy Blythe Spirit is offering, and at what prices! Looks like it might turn into a story of genuine medical fraud."

"Atta boy, Andy. I thought we might end up about there."

"And, Mister Fletcher: until two this morning I was looking into something called The Tribe. You remember you asked about something called The Tribe? Well, it looks like a helluva story—"

"That's what I'm calling about, Andy."

"What?"

"The Tribe. Expect a news break on The Tribe any minute now. What you get at first won't be the real story. Not even close. Probably won't even mention The Tribe by name."

"What's the break?"

"At a supposedly secret camp in the woods in Alabama, thirty-eight members of The Tribe just shot each other."

"Did you say, 'shot each other'?"

"It was foggy. One nut started shooting and they all started shooting. Thirty-eight dead. Among the dead is a man who called himself The Reverend Doctor Commandant Kris Kriegel."

"The escapee from the federal pen in Tomaston, Kentucky."

"The same."

"He's dead?"

"No deader than he should be."

"Which is pretty dead."

"Very dead."

"I was researching him last night. I mean, this morning. That was the clue I took from you. Kris Kriegel." Now Andy's voice was excited.

"Also escapee John Leary has finished shaking the earth."

"By the way, they recovered Juan Moreno's body yesterday. In some farmer's gully in Tennessee."

"That's nice."

"Mister Fletcher, have you got this story? I mean, of the shooting?"

"Who, me?"

"No? You haven't?"

"Andy, at ten-thirty your time, do you think you could meet someone at National Airport?"

"Sure. Who?"

"A young reporter named Jack Faoni."

"Why does that name sound familiar to me?"

"He has everything. Complete computer files on The Tribe from around the country, around the world, membership lists, lists of those targeted for assassination"—Jack grinned broadly across the car seat at Fletch—"bank accounts, their plans, personal

oᴑ◯ooᴑ◯ooᴑo

knowledge of Kris Kriegel. He's even got videotape of the shooting this morning."

"Wow!"

"All in one little plastic shopping bag."

"How? Who is this Faoni?"

"Just a kid I've been working with the last few days."

"The woman you went to see at Blythe Spirit yesterday is named Faoni."

"Yeah. I had to establish this kid's credibility. He appeared out of nowhere, you see. A complete unknown to me."

"And he's good stuff?"

"Oh, yeah," Fletch said. "I think there's good stuff in him. He'll need your help, though. Is Sally free? This tape he took in the fog will need the best editing. Obviously, it should be the lead and on the air as soon as you can manage it. Unless California falls into the sea, or something else of greater interest to more people happens."

"Yes, sir."

"I would think you'd all want to work on a longer documentary format for later, but not much later."

"Yes, sir, Mister Fletcher!"

"Faoni will have to hold some of the stuff back. That's got to be understood from the beginning. The Attorney General of the United States has had much personal input into this story."

"I understand."

"Book rights and film rights to Faoni, if he wants them. He'll be on the Air T flight from Huntsville arriving at Washington's National Airport at ten thirty-six EDT."

⊶⊶∞⊶⊶∞⊶∞

"I'll be there."

"Andy?"

"Yes, Mister Fletcher?"

"Please don't call me later. Okay? I need to get some sleep."

"Gee, Mister Fletcher. I'd never think of disturbing your sleep. Never. Not ever."

After clicking off the phone connection, Fletch handed Jack his airplane ticket. "I got this for you at two o'clock this morning in Atlanta. You even have an assigned seat."

While Jack studied his ticket, Fletch said to Jack, "A woman named Slavenka Drakulic, a victim of the most recent Balkan ethnic-cleansing wars, wrote in *The New York Times Sunday Magazine:* 'We are the war. I am afraid there is no one else to blame. We all make it possible. We allow it to happen. There is no them and us. There are no numbers, masses, categories. There is only one of us and, yes, we are responsible for each other.' "

"Got a pen and piece of paper?" Jack asked.

"In the glove compartment. Just thought that quote might add something to your story, if it fits in anywhere."

"How do you spell her name?"

"By golly. The kid can even work pen and paper!"

Fletch stopped the station wagon outside Air T's departure gate at Huntsville Airport. "I won't be going in with you, if you don't mind. Home and bed for me. Thanks for the interesting weekend."

Before getting out of the car, Jack said, "You went to Wisconsin yesterday to see my mother."

o❍oo◯ooᴏo

"She sent her best."

"How did she seem to you?"

"She kept herself concealed behind a curtain, Jack. I couldn't really see her."

"Oh."

"As astute as ever."

Jack got out of the car.

"Wait a minute," Fletch said.

On the sidewalk, Fletch unbuttoned his shirt. "You've been wearing that shirt since Friday night. Mine isn't exactly fresh, either, but at least, for the most part, I've been in air-conditioning since I put it on yesterday morning. I don't want you put off the plane because you stink even higher to heaven."

"Switch shirts?"

"Why not?"

"Here?"

"We have a choice? You don't have time to buy a new shirt."

"No. I don't."

On the sidewalk, Fletch and Jack switched shirts. Jack's shirt smelled really bad. It felt grimy.

Jack asked, "How did you know I didn't shoot at that cop? Because I didn't know how to load the gun you handed me?"

"More than that."

"What?"

"I doubt you'd attempt anything without accomplishing it. Even murder."

Fletch was within ten miles of the farm.

As soon as he could after leaving Huntsville Airport he had stopped at a truck stop for coffee. Before

∘◌∾◌∾◌◌∾◌∘

even ordering his coffee, he had bought a new shirt and thrown Jack's into a rubbish barrel.

His new T-shirt had a logo on it which read: WHY HUG THE ROAD WHEN YOU'VE GOT ME?

He had a choice of either that logo or a beer advertisement.

Fletch felt strangely lonely.

The sight of Jack heading into the airport terminal in Fletch's own shirt, carrying his plastic shopping bag full of a Big Story on disks and audio and videotapes, that silly small tattoo of a blue eye staring behind him from the top of the calf muscle of his left leg, almost winking as he walked . . . the way Jack turned before going through the circular door, grinned and waved at Fletch, knowing full well his father was watching him . . .

He was missing the kid.

Shoot. I didn't even know he existed before Friday.

Fletch found the phone on the car seat beside him and pressed the number of the farm.

Carrie answered. "Hello?"

"Hello."

"Where are you?"

"I'll be home in a few minutes."

"That's good. Hey, Fletch! Guess what?"

"What?"

"I made a firecracker cake!"

Fletch said, "Oh, boy."

o◯ooo◯ooo◯o

And now,
a special preview of *Fletch Reflected*,
the newest Fletch adventure
from Gregory Mcdonald—
available in hardcover from G.P. Putnam's Sons . . .

"Faoni." In fact, he was answering the telephone at Andy Cyst's desk in the huge Global Cable News building in Virginia. He had no desk, or telephone, of his own.

The switchboard knew he was working with Andy Cyst.

"Fletch?"

"Who is this?"

The young woman's voice said, "Is this Fletch?"

"Yeah. Jack. Faoni. Fletch."

"I know your name is Jack Faoni. The weekend we spent together you had me call you Fletch."

"When was that?"

"Skiing. In Stowe, Vermont. A few years ago. We met there. At The Shed. You were with some other guys from a lumber camp. Playing your guitar. People were buying you beer to keep you playing. Well, I sort of kidnapped you. First, I kidnapped your guitar." Her voice was low and warm. "When you pursued me to the parking lot to get your guitar back, I grabbed you. It was snowing. You were very hot. I ripped your shirt. I pulled it down off your shoulders. Do you remember the snow flakes falling on your sweating shoulders while we kissed? You sizzled."

"Good grief! Whoever you are, woman, you just elevated my temperature by more than a little. I'm hot now." Sticking a finger inside his shirt collar, Jack scanned the huge, brightly lit, colorful, air-conditioned room filled with journalists' work stations. "I wasn't a minute ago."

"You were very playful. Silly. You don't remember me?"

"I do." She had coal black hair, very wide-set coal black eyes . . . And her name was? "I remember you weren't there when I woke up."

"I had to meet my father early for Belgian waffles. It really wasn't a weekend we spent together. Just a few lonely hours."

"I remember it was a cold morning and I had to run through the snow in a flannel shirt torn to shreds. Thanks for leaving me my guitar, anyway."

"You use your hands beautifully."

"Why didn't you come back? Leave a note? Something?"

"I had to ski with my father. Then he drove me back to Poughkeepsie."

"I waited." He had not waited long. The snow was

o◯○oo◯oo◯o

pure powder, the skiing too good to miss. "I wasn't sure you weren't a dream."

"Anyway, I've been seeing your name on GCN the last few days. Those great stories about The Tribe."

"Thanks. I guess."

"You're working for GCN now?"

"I guess so. I'm here. They've used everything I've brought them."

"That's great. But they never showed your face on television. If it was your story, why didn't they use you on camera?"

"One doesn't do that."

"One doesn't? A lot do."

"People come to recognize you. Then you can't do the kind of stories I want to do."

"Oh. You must have been working on that story a long time."

"It took a long time to set up. Once it got going, it went quickly. Very quickly."

"So guess where I am."

"You like games, don't you?"

"Yeah. I do."

"Let me think . . . You're in jail?"

"No."

"You're in a hospital with some horrible disease the doctor says you must tell me about?"

"No."

"I give up." Jack rearranged some papers on Andy Cyst's desk. "Why don't you remind me of your name, if you ever shared it with me in the first place, tell me where you are, if that's relevant to the conversation, then tell me why you called. You've talked so long

○◯○○◯○○◯○

I'm beginning to need a shower."

"We didn't do all that much talking, as I remember. We went at each other like bear cubs."

"I don't care who you are. I don't care where you are. I don't care why you're calling. Good-bye."

"Staufel."

"Is that a name, or an order?"

"Shana Staufel."

"Oh, yes. Shana. So where are you, Shana?"

"Vindemia."

"Vindemia. I've read that word somewhere. What is it, defunct coal mines in Appalachia, what?"

"One of the biggest estates in America."

"Oh, yeah. In Georgia? Owned by . . ."

"Actually, I'm calling you from a phone booth outside the Vindemia Gas Station and General Store. The estate has its own little village, complete with chapel, library, and many, many rent-a-cops."

"Cute. Owned by . . . the guy who invented uh . . ."

"Chester Radliegh. He invented the perfect mirror."

"Oh, yeah. The guy who straightened out our left from our right, right from left when we look at ourselves in a mirror."

"Right. Chester Radliegh. Massive implications for industry, science, space . . ."

"You sound like you're quoting from *Business Digest*."

"I am. I looked him up. Before I met him."

"Boxers appreciate his mirror, too."

"They do?"

"They don't get blind-sided so much these days. Haven't you noticed?"

o〇oo〇oo〇o

"Guess I haven't."

"More fights go the whole ten, fifteen rounds now."

"Is that good?"

"Think of the philosophical, psychological, to say nothing of poetic ramifications of the perfect mirror. I mean, for centuries we were seeing ourselves wrong, weren't we? Not as others saw us, as they say."

"Do we ever, anyway?"

"I'd like to meet him. Radliegh must have an interesting mind. To take a thing as ancient and simple as the mirror and realize it was wrong; it was backward . . . 'In the clear mirror of thy ruling star/I saw, alas! some dread event depend.' "

"Who said that?"

"Before I did? A guy named Pope."

"I'm going to marry Chet."

"What's a Chet?"

"Chester Radliegh, Jr."

"Oh. You called to invite me to your wedding? I'll send a present. Shreds of my flannel shirt, as a keepsake, or a dust cloth, whichever you need the more."

"Not exactly."

"What then?"

"To invite you here."

"Where? Vindemia?"

"Yes."

"You need someone to speak up for you? A playmate reference, maybe?"

"This is the first time I've ever been here. I've come to meet the family."

"I don't get it. Why would you need me? Even want me in the same state?"

"You're an investigative reporter."

"Thanks."

"There's something real weird about this place. These people."

"Sure. They got very, very rich, very, very fast. Who said, 'Wealth doesn't corrupt as much as it reveals'?"

"Pope?"

"I don't think so."

"I want you to come here. I can say you're my cousin."

"As I remember, we look nothing alike."

"Sometimes cousins don't. You could just be passing by and drop in for a few days."

"Sure. You're marrying into a maxi-wealthy family, get brought home by Chet ditto to meet Mama, Papa and the Borzoi hound, and your distant relatives start landing on them asking directions to their larder. What kind of an impression would that make?"

"This place is so big, there are so many people wandering around, you wouldn't even be noticed."

"Yeah, I do a pretty good imitation of a potted palm. You telling me you think there's a story for me here somewhere? What is it? The guy's been profiled a million times. A Massachusetts Institute of Technology professor of physics invents the perfect mirror, makes zillions of dollars between a Tuesday and Friday, buys half the state of Georgia, builds a fifty-room mansion—"

"Seventy-two. Seventy-two rooms."

"Really? I thought I was exaggerating."

"The roof is five acres."

∞○○○○○○○○

"Lor' love a duck! I've been on farms smaller than that."

"Five acres, they tell me. It looks it."

"—has a gorgeous, well-behaved family—"

"That's where the profile goes awry."

"They are not a gorgeous, well-behaved family?"

"They're gorgeous." She hesitated.

"So?"

"I think they want to kill him."

"What? Who?"

"Chester Radliegh. I think his family wants to murder him. His friends. The people who work for him. Everybody around him. I'm afraid one of them will succeed."

"What on earth makes you say a thing like that? Is he that much of a bastard?"

"He's a wonderful man."

"Then why do you say such a thing?"

"I don't know, exactly. Things are weird here. Little things. Everything is so tight, you know? Security. Yet, these weird little things keep happening. I think Chester, Mister Radliegh, thinks he has invented the perfect mirror in his family, all the people he has collected around him, except they're not perfect, they seem to want to leap at him . . ."

Andy Cyst was walking from the administration offices toward his desk. The room was so big Jack thought there was a need for conveyer belts on the floor. It was not a city room; it was a world room; a cosmic room.

Jack took his feet off the edge of Andy's console desk.

o⊂⊃oo⊂⊃oo⊂⊃o

" . . . That's why I want you to come here," Shana continued. "Investigate this. There's so much tension. I'm afraid of what's going to happen."

Jack stretched the muscles of his upper back. He had had an exciting but exhausting few weeks. "Well, I'd like to meet Mister Radliegh, as I said," Jack said into the phone, "but I do have a job, I think, and you understand I can't drop everything and come to some Valhalla in the sky, pass myself off as some itinerant relation to the daughter-in-law-to-be, just in case the butler spits in daddy's mock turtle soup. You do understand that, don't you?"

"What can I do to persuade you?"

"Make me believe there's a story here."

"Is 'story' all that matters to you? I've heard you play the guitar. I've had you in bed. The whole world has just seen this wonderful exposé of The Tribe you've done. You mean to tell me you don't care about people?"

"Get some evidence. Find me a plan to collapse those five acres of roof on Chester Radliegh."

"I was hoping you'd do that. Find evidence, I mean."

"I have a life, lady."

"Lucky you."

"Give me your phone number, just in case old Chester gets carted off to the hospital with a case of botulism, or something."

She recited the main number of the estate. "There's a switchboard," she said. "I'm in the American Girl Rose suite."

Andy stepped into his workstation.

"What does that mean?" Jack asked.

o◯ooo◯ooo◯o

"The suites don't have numbers. Each is named after a particular flower, or plant. My suite is called the American Girl Rose suite."

"Ah. I see. Sounds homey enough. Does it come complete with pricks?"

"Homey enough if your last name is Windsor. Will you at least think about it?"

"I don't see how I can."

Shana Staufel sighed. "Okay. Well, it was nice meeting you. Nice talking to you."

"Best wishes," Jack said, "on your marriage."

"A story?" Andy asked.

"A girl."

Jack stood up.

"Alex Blair asked me to tell you to come to his office right away."

"Who's he?"

"His office is down the Central Corridor, right next to the CEO's." Andy sat in his chair. "He's waiting for you now."

"Okay."

"Jack?"

"Yeah?"

"You know, one of my assignments here is to answer the phone to Mister Fletcher. He's a stockholder. A director. He has a past in this business, at least print journalism, I don't know, was a respected journalist, I guess: I've heard he was; I've heard he wasn't. Sometimes he calls me three and four times a day. Then weeks will go by when I don't hear from him at all. When he has story ideas, needs some research done."

o◯ooo◯ooo◯o

"Sounds like a tough assignment."

"No," Andy said. "It's interesting. I try to figure out what he's doing, thinking, what he's working on by the questions he asks. He's very oblique. Almost never do his questions mean nothing. Usually something interesting results; sometimes something sensational. I'm learning a lot from him. I think I am. It was that way regarding The Tribe story. There were little questions in Kentucky, about a woman named Faoni. One huge story developed, and one very good story."

"This guy Blair is waiting for me."

"How did you meet Mister Fletcher, Jack? How did your paths cross?"

Jack said, "Ask him."

o◯ooo◯ooo◯o

Mirror, mirror, on the wall...

GREGORY MCDONALD

author of Son of Fletch

FLETCH REFLECTED

When Fletch's newfound son, Jack, decides to help a former lover in distress, his kindness brings him big trouble. Fresh, witty, and irreverent, this is Gregory Mcdonald at his best!

Available in hardcover at bookstores everywhere

G. P. Putnam's Sons
A member of The Putnam Berkley Group, Inc.

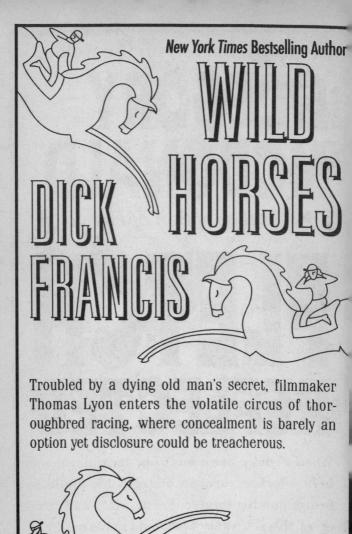